REDEMPTION TRAIL

Petty criminal Alfred Collins finds himself the victim of a conspiracy to frame him for murder. Sentenced to twenty years in prison, he manages to effect a daring escape, and assumes a new identity. Eventually he learns that the man who framed him has fled to work for a lumbering company. Consumed with the passion for revenge and the thought of being able to force a confession that would clear his name and free him from the life of a fugitive, Collins follows his trail into the Canadian wilderness . . .

VICTOR ROUSSEAU

REDEMPTION TRAIL

Complete and Unabridged

LINFORD
Leicester

First published in Great Britain

First Linford Edition
published 2018

*A catalogue record for this book is available
from the British Library.*

ISBN 978–1–4448–3828–2

Published by
F. A. Thorpe (Publishing)
Anstey, Leicestershire

Set by Words & Graphics Ltd.
Anstey, Leicestershire
Printed and bound in Great Britain by
T. J. International Ltd., Padstow, Cornwall

This book is printed on acid-free paper

1

Stepping round the corner of the rock-cutting, Alfred Collins found himself alone. Automatically he stopped working, and stood leaning upon his pick and looking towards the hills.

Those moments of solitude, few and very far between, were the most precious of all the gifts life had left for him. They were the most precious thing conceivable to a man in the first few months of a sentence of twenty years for murder in the second degree.

Especially when he was bunked in a crowded, clanging jail of steel. Especially when he was innocent.

There had been occasions since Alf had entered the state penitentiary when he had known that he was actually mad. Nearly as mad, for instance, as the two men in the infirmary who made day and night hideous with their uproar while awaiting transference to the state asylum.

1

There had been moments when only the utmost exercise of willpower had held Alf back from imitating the example furnished every few months, and leaping over the railed corridor to the flags far underneath the tier of cells in which he was confined. At such times, when long brooding had warped his brain, monstrous delusions had crept in and found lodgment there. Then the whole world seemed to be a part of the conspiracy that had railroaded him to the pen.

Those moments of despair had, however, already begun to occur less frequently; less frequent, too, the fits of sullen dreadful brooding when the universe was a black pit, a huge bowl up whose slippery sides he essayed to crawl into the sunlight, only to slip back into the darkness. Gradually he had begun to accept the incredible fact of that interminable sentence. Twenty years! He had even reckoned up that he would be forty when he came out, if he received the maximum remission.

But that was eternity. And, in general, his mind refused to accept the shock of its acknowledgment. He was convinced that he would never serve it. Either he would die, or he would go mad, or — he would make his getaway.

And that last possibility he had also refused to consider for the time. He was keeping that for the indefinite future, when he had grown calmer, craftier, when the interior of the pen had ceased to rasp his nerves like a file, when they had ceased to quiver at each unexpected sound. Yes, that was the single boon of life within that hellish iron den, that was eating into his soul — solitude. And here, round the corner of the rock-cutting, shut off from the rest of the gang by a thin ledge of rock, Alf felt as if the burden had been momentarily lifted from his shoulders.

The prisoners were working on an excavation that was being made for an extension of the building. Soon more hideous iron plates and girders would appear, and a new cage-work would arise, tier above tier, clanging and reverberating night and day.

Alf leaned upon his pick and let his

mind stray back, as it was always straying, to that man he had been, such an infinitely long time ago, before his arrest and trial.

He had been brought up on his uncle's farm, forty miles from the city, whither, when he was nine years old, his father's brother had grudgingly conveyed him, after his father and his pretty mother had died in the same week of malignant typhoid. Alf had no very deep impressions of his life before that in the city tenement apartment. He recalled his father as a factory hand, often out of a job, oftener drunk, and happily often absent for weeks together, when his mother sewed and scrubbed and some-how kept the home together. Alf had loved that New England mother of his. She had been too good for his father. He remembered the night she died . . . no; that was of the things he would not let himself remember.

So at nine years of age Alf had been carried away to his uncle's farm, and the ten or eleven years that had followed Alf looked back upon as an unmitigated hell.

A hell of hot, dirty farm work in summer. A hell of winter chores and chilblains. His uncle had been a vicious, miserly old man, his aunt a harridan. Alf grew up a weakling, the butt of other farm boys of coarser mould. All the while he was dimly conscious of certain instincts in him, derived from that New England mother of his, buried deep down in him, perhaps destined to flower someday.

He wanted, without knowing it, something better of life than this. He wanted love and understanding, and grew embittered and hopeless at not finding them. Such natures have no place on a drab farm. But there is still less place for them in a city slum. Alf had not known that before, because he had had his mother. He was to find that out.

At twenty he disappeared from the farm forever. He went to the city, drifting from one unskilled job to another. Then came a period of unemployment. Then it was Alf met the little crook, Murphy, who befriended and staked him, and introduced him to Pop Tarkle's scatter.

Alf lived there some time before he

understood what manner of men frequented it, and, being unobservant, would perhaps have taken longer if Murphy had not begun to speak about easy money. He took him around, taught him to drink, and inveigled him into a nocturnal burglary expedition in a closed house. Alf was in the room, and Murphy was blowing the safe before Alf quite understood. After that Alf felt that he had crossed the rubicon, and he no longer resisted Murphy's overtures.

Murphy spoke to him one day of Hump Egan. Hump was a link between the crooks and an organisation that acted on behalf of certain predatory interests. Alf saw Murphy in conversation with Egan, whose name was whispered as that of an all-powerful being in Pop Tarkle's scatter. Egan was built like a bull. He had graduated from the ring; a spinal curvature which in no wise detracted from his physical prowess had earned him his soubriquet. Murphy did not present Alf, who stood off and looked at this stupendous being in awe and admiration, and Egan did not deign to cast a glance in Alf's direction. Afterward Murphy explained to Alf that Egan was behind him, and that his protection guaranteed immunity in anything.

He did not hurry the boy. He just threw out a hint or two occasionally. Then he made his proposal. The story he told Alf about the old man who had been marked down was really immaterial. The essence was that he would be passing the corner of a squalid street at a certain time, when something would be pulled off, and Alf was to keep watch for the bulls. 'Easy money,' whispered Murphy.

Alf's sense of right and wrong had been pretty well blunted by this time, and how could he have suspected what a web had been woven about this simple-appearing scheme? Or, again, that he had already been marked down by the dicks as Murphy's new sidekick, which had been of the essence of the plan?

Then . . . that night. The watching at the dark corner, the sudden choked cry, the disappearing figure, the dead man lying on the sidewalk with his head in the gutter . . .

The bulls were on the spot twenty seconds later.

Of course, Alf had not the smallest chance in the world when he was put on trial.

Nevertheless, the district attorney was not quite satisfied, in the face of Alf's stolid professions of innocence. The police were baffled in their attempt either to learn something about Alf's past or to force a confession from him. So, by one of those compromises that are often made when the prisoner is a little crook, not worth too much investigation or expense, the proposal was mooted that Alf should plead guilty of murder in the second degree.

'I tell you I ain't done it!' whined Alf in his cell.

'Mebbe not, but if you don't plead second-degree murder you'll go to the gallows for sure,' said his lawyer, the little shyster who had been appointed by the court to see that justice was done to the prisoner.

'I ain't done it! I ain't done it!' Alf whined again.

'That don't make no difference,' answered the other, who, like the police and the district attorney, was anxious to have finished with Alf. 'You take my tip,' he advised. 'Plead second degree, and I'll have it all cleared up in a few weeks, and you'll find yourself a free man once more.'

The trembling gutter rat took the lawyer's advice, to the considerable satisfaction of the police and prosecution. So Alf, who would have been acquitted, had gone off to serve his sentence of twenty years' imprisonment. Three days later, if anyone had mentioned Alf to his lawyer, he would not at first have known who was referred to.

How long ago had that been? Months? Years? A few months; but it was only the change in the seasons that indicated to Alf the passage of the days. He had entered the pen through slush and snow, and it was now summer. A bird was singing somewhere. Alf leaned upon his pick and listened.

Perhaps the most hideous punishment of the pen was a psychological one. It was this: A man goes into the pen for — not twenty years, we'll say, but five, or three. He says to himself, 'I'll stick it out.' He plans to take his medicine, to pick up his life again, when he comes out, as if nothing had happened, as if for two years everything had merely been in suspense. There are things to be said, people to see, scores to be wiped out . . .

But you can't isolate yourself in time. Everything, even yourself, is changing every instant, new situations are arising, time is smoothing out old ones and creating new ones. You come out a different man, into a different world. There is a gap in your personality that can't be bridged. So you have to surrender yourself to the prison walls, to fall into step with time, and become the creature of the day and hour and moment, hoping just to be able to pick up a few threads of the past when at last you emerge.

Alf had begun to learn that lesson. He knew now that he would come out at the end of his twenty years a different being. The idea of vengeance on Murphy had worn thin. After twenty years . . .

But, still his mind refused to assimilate the meaning of that incredible sentence. And he stood there in the cutting, staring at the distant hills. The air was laden with soft, hazy moisture from the great lake behind them. There was freedom in the hills. One could hide up in safety there.

Dozens, Alf knew, had tried it; many had got away, had remained at large a day or two. Hardly one had effected a permanent escape. The roads were few, and it was several miles to the nearest town; that was why escape was practically impossible. The experience of years had shown that there was a larger, stronger cage outside that cage of clanging steel.

Behind the angle of the rock-cutting, Alf heard the men's picks digging into the rock. How long had he been standing there? Half a minute? Five minutes? In a moment Mulligan would be shouting for him. He might as well hurry back. He had had those minutes, and they had strengthened him.

The air was thickening with the mist that was creeping up imperceptibly from the lake. Already the distant hills were hidden in a haze. That meant knocking off work for the afternoon.

'Hey, git into line there!'

The guards were shouting. Alf peered round the edge of rock and saw the men tramping back from the cutting with their picks. Their figures were becoming blurred in the fog. In another moment he would be missed. He started toward them; but he stopped and looked back, and he heard the bird still singing out of the haze.

'Four twenny-four! Where's four twenny-four?'

Well, why not?

With a sudden, uncontrollable impulse, Alf glided back and reached the road, hearing shouting behind him; the next moment he was in the heart of the fog and racing, panting, straining toward the hills.

2

It was in the fall, a little more than four years later, that Alf found himself in the city again.

He had made the most sensational escape in the records of the state penitentiary, and he had effected it by an inspiration that was genius.

His natural, primary impulse had been to travel as fast and far as possible. That is the instinctive impulse. That is the fatal impulse. In the instinctive reliance upon one's physical means of locomotion, one forgets that the telephone works nearly one hundred and five million times as fast as a man can run. Alf could never have made his getaway like that.

The germ of Alf's idea had been his remembering reading in the newspapers of a prisoner in an Irish jail who had starved himself to death. He had lived without food for ninety days

Knowing that he was safe so long as he

remained in the hills, Alf had hidden in a cave that he had stumbled on, once the lair of some animal.

He had lain there fifteen days. Fifteen days without food, and with nothing but water from a spring. Fifteen days without a covering and without fire, crouching like the hunted beast that he was, actually within easy sound of the penitentiary bell, while he was hunted far and wide. Every morning, when the sun rose among the hills opposite and grinned into his cave, awakening him, Alf had made a notch upon a piece of wood.

At the end of the fifteen days a reconnaissance showed Alf that the guards had been withdrawn from the roads. Alf proceeded by night to a small lake some distance away, with summer cottages all round it, still unoccupied. He broke into two, and in the second found an old fishing suit. He put it on and buried his convict clothes in the woods. He discovered the name of the man who owned the cottage from an old addressed envelope, and later sent him fifteen dollars. Alf intended to run straight, but he did not know that this was the New England mother in him. It was a fad to which he adhered grimly, without conviction or principle; but he meant to fight his way through life untrammeled by any other weaknesses.

He made his way to the city and took a job at an employment agency, which sent him across the northern border to a lumber camp. And as a lumberjack, in one camp or another, Alf spent the four ensuing years.

Being intelligent, he soon learned a good deal about the business. Having in mind the single purpose of someday establishing his innocence, as a preliminary to success, and because of that something in him which had enabled him to pass unscathed through Pop Tarkle's scatter, Alf emerged at the end of those four years a very different being from the gutter rat who had cringed in the dock and pleaded guilty to second-degree murder in order to escape the gallows.

He had graduated in the rough school of life. He had learned to look the world in the face and to hold his own among men. He had even educated himself, with the purpose of fitting himself for better things. He was in passionate revolt against the man who he had been.

He had learned the lesson of life, that to the strong all things are permissible, and that there is no greater sin than of weakness. By aid of that lesson, he meant someday to rise to power.

It was the unexpected bankruptcy of the company with which he was engaged as foreman, and the loss of half a winter's wages, that threw him on his beam-ends. Alf saw nothing but to go back to the city and look for another job. He had no fear of detection. He had grown, filled out — he looked an altogether different man.

And yet he was recognised before he had been in town two hours. Outside the labour agency to which he had made his way in order to apply for a job, he came face to face with Murphy. He was unchanged, and Alf knew him immediately; but it was not until he had stared grimly into the little crook's face for several seconds that Alf saw the dawn of recognition there.

Alf beckoned Murphy round the corner, and Murphy obeyed in terror.

'Well, what you got to say?' demanded Alf.

'Say, Alf, you got me wrong fer sure!' Murphy whined.

'I've nothing to say about you beating it while you had the chance. But you'd planned to croak him and you fixed the frame-up on me.'

Although he did not know it, Alf's hands were jerking up toward Murphy's throat. Murphy knew that if they closed, their grip would be unbreakable.

'Listen, Alf, fer Gawd's sake!' he whined. 'I didn't frame you up. I swear I didn't. It was Hump Egan. He fixed the job. I was to slug the old gink, and you was to come along. I didn't know Hump was framing us both.'

'What's that?' demanded Alf.

'I didn't soak him. I never knew nothin' till I got there half a minute after the bulls pinched you and saw the crowd, and him lyin' in the road.'

Alf's hands went up, not to Murphy's

throat, but to his shoulders. Alf shook Murphy to and fro till his head nodded drunkenly on his shoulders.

'What did you get out of it?'

'Not a cent, Alf, I swear I didn't. Hump reneged on me.'

'You say he framed you up?'

'Sure, both of us,' said Murphy, beginning to recover confidence. 'He'd got a third party to touch off that old gink, and he was layin' pipes to railroad you and me to the gallows.'

Alf released Murphy and swore under his breath. He believed the little gutter rat, chiefly because the trick seemed to him beyond Murphy's powers of planning and carrying out.

'Where's Hump?' he demanded.

'Hump's beat it. He ain't ben round these parts since then. Guess it was gettin' a bit too warm fer him.'

'Where's he gone?'

'He was up in Canady somewheres, workin' fer the Sorel & Smith Lumber Company last thing I heard of him. I ain't seen him in years, and I've ben runnin' straight. That's straight goods, Alf!'

Alf considered. '*Beat it!*' he commanded suddenly.

Murphy, whose nerve was badly shaken, made haste to obey. Alf watched him as he departed, and then started off in the opposite direction.

He walked fast and far, deep in thought. He had always concluded that there had been a frame-up, if only from the fact that Egan had deserted him at the trial; but somehow he had considered Murphy, not Egan, as his betrayer. Now he saw that it was Egan with whom he had to settle.

And the settlement had to come, and he was less concerned with wringing Egan's neck than with forcing a confession from him. He would have given everything, except his liberty, to wipe out his record. Recapture might be remote, but so long as he remained a fugitive from the law he would feel himself an Ishmael. That distant threat, even though it never materialised, warped his life, paralysed his initiative, and hindered him from becoming the man he meant someday to be.

It was extremely improbable that Egan

would know him, even if he had looked at him that day they met. But Egan had not cast a glance at him. Alf felt confident that if he could find Egan, he would pass with him for a stranger.

Alf resolved to find Egan, and, if he were lumbering, to get a job in the same camp and bend all his energies to discovering whatever was to be learned. No pertinacity would be too great, no labour too arduous.

He soon discovered that the Sorel & Smith Company was a small concern with limits at Lake St. Laurent, on the Quebec-Ontario boundary, and that, in common with many of the Canadian camps, it was recruiting labourers. Alf found out the local agent and applied for a job.

The agent looked him over, discovered that he was not the usual type of casual applicant, and modified the brusqueness with which he had at first greeted him. 'Had any experience?' he asked.

'Four years,' said Alf. 'Teamster, swamper, cant-hook, sawyer — most everything except cookee.'

'Where?'

Alf told him, giving the name Alfred Collet, under which he had worked — a French name, common in parts of the north.

'French, eh? Speak the language?'

'Sure, it was my father's,' answered Alf.

The agent sized him up again. It was obvious to him that Alf had his own reasons for wanting to get north, and the agent put his own deductions on that fact. Skilled lumberjacks did not usually apply for jobs in Canada, where the pay was smaller than in their own country, especially with the current shortage of labour.

'Guess you wouldn't be too sorry to get over the boundary for a spell?' he asked with a significant smile.

Alf admitted it, and, an understanding being thus effected, the agent forthwith became confidential. 'The Sorel & Smith Company's got a standing order for me,' he said, 'and can't get them. There's been some trouble up to their camp. I understand there's a bunch of Canuck squatters trying to hold up their work,

21

and starting strikes, and so on. They want half a dozen roughnecks to go up there and help put that gang out of business if they get funny again. How about that?'

'Suits me,' said Alf.

'I don't know nothing about the pay. You know they don't pay as high up there as here. I furnish transportation, and you make your arrangements when you get there, and you can take it or leave it.'

Alf agreed to this one-sided proposition in a way which left the agent more convinced than ever that he had his own reasons for wanting to get away in a hurry. The understanding effected, the agent told him to meet him that evening at the Union Station.

Alf met him there at the appointed time. Ranged behind him he saw five of the toughest-looking specimens that he had come across since Pop Tarkle's days lined up with disreputable bundles. All were French-Canadians, and all looked like the lowest class of jailbird.

'Think you can hold that lot?' the agent grinned.

'I guess so,' answered Alf.

'All right, you're boss,' said the agent. 'This man's your boss, comprenny?' he informed the men, who grinned back.

'Where d'you pick 'em up?' asked Alf.

'Say, they ain't what you might call good-looking,' said the agent, 'but they was all there was on the market, and the company wanted men who could speak the language. Well, they're roughnecks for sure, and that's what they're asking for. Here's your train ready.'

Alf pondered over things for a long time that night, as the train sped northward, in the intervals of trying to snatch a little sleep. He had not ventured to ask if Egan was with Sorel & Smith. That would have been too dangerous. And he meant to proceed with infinite caution.

It was so thin a clue. But it was a possibility, and, with care, Alf dreamed of someday picking up the thread of what had happened that night at the corner of the squalid street. Meanwhile, if Egan were not at present employed in the camp, it was at least the place where

Alf had the best chance of learning of his whereabouts.

Alf dozed fitfully through the night. Toward morning, after the train had passed the boundary, the stops became more frequent. There were the numerous little way-stations with sleepy agents and night-travelling farmers and drummers that Alf knew, so well. It was in a measure like returning home, and he grew more contented. Slowly the grey light began to filter into the car, revealing the unshaven faces of three of the gang, lolling against each other in the opposite seat, and snoring.

Alf tapped one of the men on the knee, and he awoke with a ludicrous start of terror that aroused his companions also.

'Where's the other two?' Alf asked.

Broad grins met his interrogations. Finally he learned that two of the men had got off the train at stations just across the Canadian border.

Alf swore. However, he did not feel the responsibility that the agent had thrust upon him. Nevertheless, he kept a

24

watchful eye upon the three whenever the train stopped. None of them attempted to slip away, however, until they changed stations at Montreal, when one of the three dodged across the platform and took to his heels.

The gang being thus reduced to two, Alf took one by either arm and so paraded them through the streets to the terminal. At noon he had them at St. Joseph, the end of the line, from which point there was a twenty-mile drive by rig to Lake St. Laurent.

A down-train was standing in the station, just about to start back for Montreal. As it began to move, one of the remaining pair broke free, dashed across the metals, and scrambled up the steps of a car, from which a moment later he was impudently kissing his hand to Alf.

This left Alf with just one survivor of the gang. Alf looked him over. He was a bleary little gin-soaked rat with red-rimmed eyes. The rat looked back at Alf and grinned.

With a sudden impulse of disgust, Alf shot out his foot and kicked him to the edge of the platform. '*Beat it!*' he commanded.

The rat obeyed.

3

The defection of Alf's travelling companions was not without its compensation, for, probably through some misunderstanding, the conveyance that was in waiting at St. Joseph station consisted of a rig with only a single seat, beside the driver.

All through the glowing afternoon, Alf sat beside the old, taciturn, gray-bearded Frenchman, who drove his rat-tailed bay along the narrow endless road, up and down hills of incredible grade, clothed in a virgin forest. In the balmy balsam-scented air, Alf felt the burden of the past slipping away. His encounter with Murphy, which had usurped the forefront of his consciousness, reviving all the latent bitterness of past years, became relegated to its normal place. The hope of finding Egan became more of an incident in the search for employment.

Those four years that Alf had spent in the woods had, in fact, sunk deep into his spirit. They had drawn him to them and made him of them. All the past he had known — the city slum, the farm, Pop Tarkle and the penitentiary — had become an evil, unsubstantial dream. Alf felt that he was back where he belonged; he had come home.

And as always at such times of returning, one figure, that of his mother, stood out with unblemished purity and light. There was, too, some conflict between that figure and his resolve to accomplish his ends without scruple. Alf was conscious of this conflict, which he had never got to the point of analysing; some day, he knew, it would present itself to him as a matter for instant choice.

Two or three times upon the road he tried to draw the old man out upon the subject of the Sorel & Smith Company, with questions put in various ways, but he found himself unable to break his monosyllabic reticence, and at last he desisted and sat back and resigned himself to the enjoyment of his surroundings.

Late in the afternoon, the gleaming blue waters of Lake St. Laurent appeared in the distance, a long curving sheet of water glistening in the hollow of the hills, a brimming cup in the cool depths of the forest. Now they began to pass through a region that had already been lumbered. The dead stumps of the pines and spruces stood up, bare and gaunt, but already the ferns and creeping plants were draping them. The blueberry shrubs were touched with frost, their berries fallen, but here and there gleamed the bright scarlet of the pigeonberry, and the birch and maple were just beginning to flame among the evergreens. A partridge with her brood half-grown scurried out of the way, fluttering before the rig and feigning a broken wing. Alf saw deer-cropping upon the bark of trees. A hare, with the first white mottling of winter, in her fury leaped across the trail into the undergrowth.

They passed a burned-out blackened cabin in a small clearing, the timbers of the charred roof fallen into the interior, the windows set like sightless eyes on each side of the gaping doorway. It was the picture of desolation, that lonely blackened cabin, with the forest seemingly pressing in on it from all sides, as if to hide it.

Alf pointed to the ruins. 'Folks had a fire, looks like,' he said.

The old driver bit viciously upon his pipe, but did not answer him. A curve of the trail concealed the ruins. But at another bend of it, two more burned-out cabins came into sight. They were some distance apart and on opposite sides of the road, and Alf was puzzled as he looked at them. It seemed impossible for the flames to have leaped from one cabin to the other, even with the most furious gale, for they were not only a good way apart, but each was set some distance back in a small clearing.

Alf turned to the driver again. 'Folks in these parts seem to be mighty careless about fires,' he said.

The driver still maintained his silence. But when at the next turn of the road they passed a fourth burned cabin, Alf turned to the old man beside him in more insistent interrogation. The driver deliberately pulled in his horse. He took his pipe out of his mouth and laid it down. He turned to Alf.

'*You think you make game of me, eh, monsieur?*' he shouted.

'Not that I know of,' answered Alf. 'Say, how d'you expect a stranger in these parts to know about your houses burning down?'

The driver stared at him. 'You don't *know*, eh?' he shouted. 'Then I tell you, my friend, *I tell you!*' And a stream of wild invective poured from his lips, accompanied by furious gestures. At first it was difficult to make anything out of what the old man was saying, but Alf soon began to get the drift of it. He gathered that this was the work of the Sorel & Smith Company, which had turned the inhabitants off its territory and deliberately set fire to their homes.

'My house, *that one!*' shouted the old man, sweeping his arm toward the blackened ruins. 'I pass it every time I drive along this road, and it keeps me from forgetting. Thirty-five years I lived there, and now my roof is burned over my head. Thirty-five years a free man, and now I must work for the company in my old age, and live, me and my wife, in the miserable shack they give me. I work with my span of horses for two dollars a day, and the food of the horses to be provided out of that. *Nom de Dieu*, two dollars a day and feed my own horses! I can stint myself, I can stint my old wife, *but a man cannot stint his horses*.'

'Say, that sounds bad,' said Alf. 'Didn't you own the land you built on?'

The driver struck his breast. '*No, no!*' he shouted. '*Nobody* owned his land. We thought *we* did. *They cheated us!*'

He caught Alf by the arm. '*Listen*, my friend!' he cried. 'I see you do not know. I shall tell you. All this land our master owned, as his father had owned it, and his father's father. Auguste Sorel was his agent, his servant. He saw that our master, old Monsieur Edouard, was not shrewd in business and trusted everyone, and he coveted his land, and wished to get it away from him, and himself become the master. Our master trusted Auguste Sorel, and let him manage all his affairs for him, and when he wished for money Sorel would give him some, and the master asked no questions. But by and by the time came when Monsieur Edouard asked for some more money, and Auguste Sorel told him that it was all gone.

' 'You must sell your land,' Auguste Sorel told him, and he said that in the United States there was a man who would buy the land. Monsieur Edouard did not know it, but this was Auguste Sorel himself, who had robbed Monsieur Edouard right and left for years.

'Monsieur Edouard swore he would never sell, but the time came when he had to do so. And he went to the United States and never came back; he was taken ill there and died of a stroke, they said, but I know it was his heart that broke. And so Auguste Sorel and this man Smith, they own these lands, and burn our homes.

'And it is our own fault, monsieur. For, five years ago, before Monsieur Edouard sold his lands he came to every one of us and said, 'My friend, you have lived here for twenty, thirty, forty years, as it may be, but all the while this is my land on which you are living. Now I am impoverished,' he said, 'and I may have to sell, and those who buy, they may perhaps turn you off the land if they see fit to do so. So you must take out patents, each one of you, and then the land becomes your own forever.'

'So we go to a man, a lawyer, who tells us that he will take out our patents for us. Ten, twenty, thirty dollars he charges us, each one of us differently, as much as we are able to pay. And he swindles us. He takes our money and tells us he has registered our parents, and that the land is now our own, but it is a lie, for he has done nothing at all.

'We knew nothing of this monsieur. We thought we owned the land. By and by the company comes. It demands rent of us, and we refuse to pay. We laugh at it. For who is this company? Auguste Sorel, and the Yankee Smith. Auguste Sorel, who worked for our master since he was a boy, and did what he told him. And what was he? A *habitant*, no better than any of us. Now, because he has become so big, he hates us, he hates to see us and to be reminded that he is no better than we are.

'And the Yankee Smith, he has no pity. To him we are like the beasts. And we all know it is because he cannot get Mademoiselle Camille, our master's daughter, that he urges Sorel to destroy our homes, for she still looks on us as her people, and it wounds her. But what can we do? She is a woman, she cannot protect us; and Monsieur Philippe, her brother, he is not the man his father, our old master was. No, we can do nothing.

'And so, because we will neither pay rent nor work for the company at the miserable wages they offer us, they burn our homes and leave us without roofs to our heads, so that we must either work or live in the woods like the beasts. Well, we strike. All last winter we strike for more money. We go cold and hungry, we take each other into those homes that are left, but we will not cut. But when the spring comes we are finished. We have to go to work. But there is no work, for the snow has gone, and there is no wood to be put through the mill, and there can be no cutting till this winter.

'So we go into debt, all of us, more debt than we can pay off in years, for what do they give us? Homes, shacks on the company land, and food, and seventy-five cents a day. What is seventy-five cents a day to a man with a family, or two dollars a day for me and my old wife when I have fed my horses? *Diable*, a man cannot stint his horses! But the end is not yet — no, no, there *will* come a day of reckoning!'

He stopped and looked suspiciously at Alf. 'But *you* — who are you, and how do you come to work for the company, with their slave-driving and their burnings, and do not know *this?*' he demanded.

4

Without waiting for Alf to answer him, the old man turned away, picked up his pipe, and relit it. Alf felt extremely uncomfortable. If this story was true, then he was in for a dirty business.

Alf cared very little about the rights and wrongs of the case, but he had envisaged his fight as against the rich, not against the poor and oppressed. Nor did he relish being used as another man's whip, which was evidently the company's purpose. He had been Egan's whip.

He brooded sullenly while the driver started his horse again, and the rig began to traverse the curving border of the lake, until suddenly the head appeared in the distance. Here, upon a flat tongue of land, projecting beneath a range of forest-clad hills of wild grandeur, curved in the shape of an elongated horseshoe, was visible the mill and settlement of the Sorel & Smith Company. As the rig approached it, Alf could discern the rushing stream that emptied itself into Lake St. Laurent, the dam and the boom, the stables and the workshops, store and office building, and a row of ramshackle huts that evidently housed the workers. Some distance up the hillside was a more substantial-looking building, presumably the abode of the partners, or one of them.

The company was evidently operating in a small way, to judge from the appearance of the plant. The peeled and cross-sawn logs were being floated down the stream for conveyance to a pulp-mill, for stray logs were stranded round the shores of the lake, and there were lines of chips upon the sandy border. A flume came into sight, winding like a centipede down from the woods toward the water.

This tongue of land was littered with tin cans and refuse. Stray curs, prowling there, yelped at the horse and scuttled away. Two or three women stood in the doorways of the huts. A few children were playing in the dust. A group of three men were standing on the stoop in front of the mean-looking store. The driver deposited

Alf and his duffle there, and, ostentatiously turning his back upon the group without a word, drove off toward the stable.

Alf stood in front of the store, inspecting these three. One, who appeared to be the storekeeper, was a stunted young Frenchman. But his companions were of such remarkable appearance that Alf looked at them for several seconds without stirring. One was a huge old Frenchman of perhaps sixty years with a long iron-grey beard. He was hardly six feet in height, but his tremendous girth gave him the aspect of phenomenal size. It was muscle, not fat; evidence of enormous strength. But more remarkable was the ferocity of the man's features. He looked like a human gorilla: the heavy beard grew up to the sunken sockets of the little eyes, and from between them curved a nose like a parrot's beak. As he opened his mouth to spit, he disclosed two long yellow fangs like an old hound's.

The younger man beside him was, from the resemblance, evidently his son. He was of the same massive build and the same ferocious aspect, tempered, however, with something more vulpine and less bovine. As Alf stood there, both of them turned to glance at him, and Alf asked the little storekeeper for Monsieur Sorel.

The man, for answer, jerked his thumb toward the door of the little office that adjoined the store. Alf started toward it, but at that moment the door opened and Sorel emerged. He was a man nearer sixty than fifty, bent, meagre, with long grey hair falling over his forehead. The face was deeply lined, furtive and cunning: the face of a small schemer, a petty, quibbling tradesman; the face of the *habitant* who has acquired money or power by underhand means. It was a face seen in the slums of the American city as well, and familiarised to Alf by his experiences. Sorel raised his head, glanced keenly at Alf out of a pair of puckered blue eyes, and went past, ignoring him.

The two Frenchmen started toward him. Sorel took one by either arm and the three started away, Sorel, between them, walking with a curious shuffling movement. Laughter came back to Alf's ears.

Alf deposited his duffle upon the stoop of the store and sat down. The little storekeeper disappeared inside the building. The heads of the three were wagging busily. They turned about and came back, the two employees guffawing loudly as Sorel expounded on something. Abreast of the cabin again, Sorel detached himself from his two companions and went back toward the store. Alf rose.

'My name's Collet,' he said. 'I'm one of the men your agent sent up yesterday for a job.'

'*Hein?* Where are the rest of you?' The puckered eyes were searching Alf's; under the wrinkled lids they looked like two very bright blue beads.

'Got away on the road,' Alf answered. 'The last one bolted when we got to St. Joseph.'

'*Hein*, the poor devils wanted to get back to their homes. That agent is always sending me up those gutter rats who are no good. The Papineaus and my foreman can handle all the damned *habitants* in this district.' Sorel was turning away.

Alf intercepted him. 'How about a job for me?' he asked.

'*Hein?* What can you do?'

'I've had four years' experience in lumber camps,' said Alf.

Sorel looked him up and down. 'I cannot pay American wages,' he answered. 'The times are hard, very hard.'

Alf said in French: 'I'd be willing to work cheap.'

'You speak French, *hein?*'

'Why, yes, more or less.'

Alf saw that a swift, almost instantaneous, and quite inscrutable process of cogitation was going on in Sorel's brain. Again the beady blue eyes bored into his. 'Come into the office, Collet,' he said after a moment of reflection.

Alf accompanied him inside the little place. It was a small wooden shanty containing very little except a desk with the office books on it, a couple of hard chairs, and a large unlighted stove.

Sorel's attitude suddenly became discreet. 'My agent, he told you what sort of work you might be wanted for?' he inquired.

'Why, he did give me to understand there was some kind of trouble up here with the people,' answered Alf.

Again Sorel studied him. 'Yes, we have had some difficulty with the squatters. The agent told you that, *hein?* It is unfortunately necessary to teach these damned *habitants* a lesson now and again. But I have enough men to handle them — Mr. Smith, my partner, and the two Papineaus are quite sufficient to keep these dogs in their own place.' He spoke malignantly; and then he shot a smile at Alf about as significant as the smile with which the agent had favoured him. And Alf smiled back in just the right sort of deprecating way. 'You, why do you wish to work here at the small wages that I can afford to pay?' Sorel demanded. 'No, do not tell me. I do not want to hear lies. You know your own business best, and no doubt you have good reasons for seeking employment so far away from your own country, *hein, hein?*'

Alf made a sort of tacit assent. Sorel was playing into his hand.

'Are you loyal?' demanded Sorel suddenly. 'For there might be a place here for a man who would be faithful to me. An American whom I could rely upon.'

There was now a sub-note of a peculiar nature in Sorel's voice, and Alf's mind leaped to it. Alf was watching Sorel now as closely as Sorel was watching him. And Alf knew that vocal note of old. It was one that he had frequently heard used by humbler men in Pop Tarkle's scatter; it was the challenge of one crook to another to give the countersign of his profession; and Alf's ears were just as keen to those subtle inflections as in the city in the days of his outlawry.

'For you appear to be a man of intelligence, Collet,' Sorel continued, 'and I like to have intelligent men about me. Intelligent men whom I know I can trust. You understand?'

Alf nodded eagerly. He would have understood anything just then for the opportunity to remain in Sorel's employment until he had discovered what he wanted to know. He could not avoid showing his eagerness, but Sorel misunderstood it. His blue eyes bored into Alf's again.

'So you think you like to work for me, *hein?*' he asked. 'If you were put on the payroll, you would remember that you were under obligations of loyalty and secrecy to me?'

'I certainly would, Mr. Sorel, and I guess you can trust me to the limit,' answered Alf. And now in turn he contrived to throw into his voice that subtle inflection universally understood among men of the Sorel mould.

A shrieking siren sounded at the mill. Sorel rose. 'Then I shall speak to my partner and see if there is a place for you, Collet,' he said.

He went out. Alf stood at the door of the office, wondering what had been in Sorel's mind, and trying to size up the situation. He saw the two brutes of Frenchmen loitering nearby. Jealous already of Sorel's interest in Alf, the pair shot black glances at him. But Alf looked away from them toward the little group that was crossing the terrain from the mill. Sorel had accosted one of these men, and they were coming back together.

And as Alf's gaze fell upon Sorel's companion, his heart gave a great bound. Well Alf knew that bull figure with the humped shoulder and the prehensile arms.

'Mr. Smith' was Hump Egan.

5

Alf's sleep that night was destined to be almost as broken as it had been the night before. In the first place, it was sheer elation that kept him awake — elation at this successful termination of his journey.

It was really most incredible. The chances had been heavy enough against Egan's still being with the Sorel & Smith Company; but to find Egan masquerading under another name, and one of the partners', was staggering in its complexity. Here was the ex-ward boss, prizefighter and gangster, transformed from the city crook into the lumberman. More than that, Egan had developed — but he had developed exactly as one might have expected such a man to develop. He had improved his grammar, but not his manners; broadened his mind, but not his character. The cheap crook had simply developed into the bigger crook.

Egan had walked up to Alf and looked him over with a scrutiny that took in every detail of him. And under that scrutiny Alf had not flinched, though it had put him on the rack. Old memories of Pop Tarkle's days, long put by, rose up in him as Egan's cold eyes traversed his face. If Egan had recognised him then, Alf would have done his best to kill him.

But of course Egan had not recognised him, and Alf knew there had never been any danger of it. And the fact that he had not done so gave Alf a feeling of immense advantage over him.

Alf had signed on as a lumberjack at seventy-five cents day. And he had fancied that that queer hint of an understanding had again been conveyed to him by Sorel's intonation as he put his signature to the paper. That was one of the things Alf was wondering about as he tossed that night upon the camp bed in the ramshackle little cabin at the end of the half-empty row of shacks; what ulterior purpose Sorel had had in mind in engaging him.

Alf was confident that some process

had been going on in Sorel's mind. And he was laying his plans as he tossed and turned in his bed. He meant to spare no effort to discover what Egan knew and force him to acknowledge it. Whoever it was had killed the unknown old man who had been buried in the Potter's Field, Egan knew. And Alf meant to wring that confession from him. By craft, by cunning, by infinite care, by cringing, by fawning, or by violence, or by all these. No scruple should stand in his way.

In one respect, 'Mr. Smith' was still the old-time gangster — in his fondness for low company. Egan occupied a bunk-house, a small structure near the mill, with his henchmen, the Papineaus, whom he seemed to treat as boon companions. The three ate in a small cookhouse adjoining, and Alf had taken his supper there. The names of the Papineaus were Aristide, the father, and Alphonse, the son; and a closer inspection of this villainous pair did not improve the estimate that Alf had formed of them. They were plainly disconcerted by his arrival, and the glances with which they favoured him were actively unfriendly.

Egan told Alf to take the empty shack at the end of the row, and unexpectedly appeared there later in the evening. This was Alf's first chance to study the man as he was. Viewed from his own developed viewpoint, the dreaded Hump Egan, of whom Pop Tarkle's inmates had spoken as a sort of god, was just a cheap, common crook. Alf swiftly realised the progress he himself had made when he saw how Egan had shrunk in his estimation; he anticipated no difficulty in handling him.

Egan had brought in a bottle of hooch with him, and immediately disclosed the object of his visit. He welcomed Alf heartily as a fellow American, and began a line of questioning which betrayed a good deal of nervousness. In fact, he suspected that Alf had been sent up by some of his old associates, and was a detective, amateur or professional. He was, at any rate, manifestly disturbed, and pumped Alf till he was satisfied with the recounting of an invented past whose composition amused Alf extremely.

'Say, that's all very well, what you tell

me about your folks in Maine, Collet,' Egan blurted out finally. 'But what I'm gettin' at is, what's your reason for comin' up here for a job?'

'Why, I was down and out, Mr. Smith,' said Alf, 'and I went into the agency, and they sent me here. They didn't say nothing about the wage, and I don't see no difference between this country and the U.S.'

'Oh, there's a *hell of a lot of difference*,' said Egan sardonically. 'Say, you jest see if you can't think up some better reason than that.'

'Why, I — I ain't got no particular reason, Mr. Smith,' insisted Alf, putting on a hang-dog expression.

'Come on, *spill it*!' demanded Egan. 'I ain't goin' to blow the game. Got into trouble, I guess, didn't you? What was it you done?'

'I ain't a crook,' whined Alf. 'You write to where I worked last, and they'll tell you I been runnin' straight.'

Egan stretched out a long arm and gripped Alf by the shoulder. 'You come through with it, Collet,' he shouted. 'You come clean, and your job here won't come to no harm. What was it you wanted to git away from America for?'

'Why, it was a little job with a peterman I got mixed up with,' Alf confessed. 'I didn't want to go in with him, but he told me he'd spill on me for something he knew about me, years before, if I didn't agree.'

'So that's why you guessed it would be healthier in Canada for a spell, Collet,' mused Egan, apparently completely hoodwinked.

'And I didn't get a cent out of it.'

Egan looked at him with vast relief. 'Well, that's all right, boy,' he said. 'I guess nobody here wouldn't hold that against you. Go on and tell me some more.'

He drained his tin mug and filled Alf's again, and Alf drank. That was the purpose of the hooch, to loosen Alf's tongue, and Alf let it wag freely and foolishly, in the manner of the weakling that he had once been, conscious that no amount of hooch could kill that cold, resolute thing in him which was the embodiment of all his sufferings in the past, and was to guard him against mistakes and weaknesses in future. So, playing his part of an ex-crook, he chattered, while Egan listened complacently, and believed he had established a complete moral ascendancy over him.

'So you think you're goin' to like this job, huh?' Egan inquired.

'Why, it's mighty poor wages, Mr. Smith,' Alf bleated. 'But when a guy's on the rocks he can't afford to be particular.'

Egan grinned. Again the long prehensile arm shot forth, and the hand gripped Alf's shoulder. 'Collet, see here! You stick to the firm, and you'll be all right. Get me?' He drained his glass and refilled it. 'You ain't drinkin',' he said to Alf with a sudden snarl of suspicion.

Again Alf drank, and still he felt as if he had drunk so much water. But it was Egan who was affected, just enough to betray himself in the slightly exaggerated movements, the loss of complete muscular self-control, just enough to unlock his lips a little too far. He leaned toward Alf confidentially. 'Now I'll give you a tip,

Collet,' he said. 'This firm's Sorel & Smith, ain't it? Well, you c'n jest fergit about the Sorel part, because it's the Smith part that counts, and it's the Smith part's goin' to count fer more and more as time goes by. Get that?'

Alf nodded and gaped. Egan scrutinised him, squinting at him through narrowing eyelids, with the sudden suspicion that he might have said too much. But Alf was looking at him with just the right amount of feigned surprise, and Egan fell for it. And Alf laughed, deep down inside him, for things were coming his way.

'Oh, I guess I got a few irons in the fire, Collet,' Egan sniggered, 'and if you're wise you'll know where the mazuma lies. Know where I got Auguste Sorel?'

'No. Where?' asked Alf vacuously.

'In here,' laughed Egan, slapping his trouser pocket. 'Oh, he was a smooth bird, the way he got these lands. But he'll get his. You jest remember that when you're sober, Collet, and you'll find yourself on velvet. What I say here goes.'

Once more Alf nodded. Egan looked a

repulsive leering satyr as he crouched in his chair, with his hanging arms. He peered narrowly into Alf's eyes. Alf let his eyes drop. Egan, grinning, caught Alf by the chin and turned his face toward his. It was an act that must have inevitably brought a blow from any normal man. But Alf did nothing, and Egan's grin grew wider.

'I guess you and me understand each other now, Collet,' Egan snickered. Satisfied, he rose and shambled out of the shack without the formality of a farewell, leaving Alf white and shaken with suppressed passion.

But Alf had learned self-discipline and infinite patience in the penitentiary, and he could afford to be patient until the reckoning. And already so much had happened, so much more than he had dared to hope for when he set out upon his journey.

The most notable thing was the desire of both Egan and Sorel to use him for their own ends, whatever these might be. Each thought him a crook, and a serviceable one; that was quite clear. Alf had noticed that Egan appeared to have some sort of ascendancy over Sorel, even during the brief time that he had seen the two together that afternoon. And Alf had seen what he felt sure Egan had not seen: Sorel's slumbering hatred toward him.

If Egan had been implicated with Sorel in some dishonesty, that would account for everything. And yet it was difficult to see how Egan could have reached forth from the slums of Fall City and possessed himself of a partnership in the limits.

Time would disclose the truth. Meanwhile, Alf had only to go on as he had begun. He had already discovered Egan without being recognised; and Egan, thinking he had a secure hold on Alf through his confession of the burglary that had never occurred, had shown his hand.

It was all these things that caused Alf to sleep badly that night. He fell asleep at last, toward morning, to dream that he was back in the penitentiary, and to start up thankfully out of that dream toward sunrise, when he was awakened by the sounds in the adjacent shacks whose family life had no more privacy than was provided by the thin partitions of pine-plank.

6

He flung his clothes on quickly and made his way to the cookhouse, where the Papineaus and Egan had already gathered. The two Frenchmen scowled darkly at Alf as they wolfed down their food, bacon and beans, and enormous flapjacks provided by the little Frenchman at the skillet. Egan welcomed Alf with a surly nod, and the four ate in silence.

'Think you c'n boss that gang today?' demanded Egan presently.

'I guess I could, Mr. Smith,' Alf answered.

'C'mon, then,' growled Egan, leading the way from the cookhouse across the terrain.

A small gang of men was getting ready to start for the woods. They were gathering sullenly into line, their wives standing in the doorways, watching them. Egan came hustling up to them.

'*Hey there*, git a move on!' he bellowed.

The men jostled more quickly into place. It was startling to Alf, with his knowledge of the lumberjack, the most independent man on earth, to see this attitude of the slave-driver assumed and accepted. Nevertheless, there were scowling looks directed at Egan as he went down the line. It was quite plain that the relationship between the company and the men was one of force and necessity.

Egan came up to Alf. 'This scum's tamed now so's it will eat out of your hand,' he said. 'See that fat old guy? That's Pascal. Three months ago Pascal had a farm, a pair of horses, and a cow. We burned him out, and both his horses got burned in the stable, because he was too stubborn to git 'em out, and now he's glad to work for his food and seventy-five a day like the rest of 'em. Hey, Pascal, *comment ça va?*' he shouted.

Pascal, a stout elderly man with a short grey beard, looking very much more like a farmer than a lumberjack, scowled at his tormentor.

'Find lumberin' easier than runnin' a farm, hey, Pascal?' jeered Egan.

For a moment Pascal's hands twitched. Then they dropped to his sides, and Pascal turned his head away.

'Say, you sons of guns, this man Collet here's your straw-boss today!' Egan shouted. 'You got to treat 'em rough,' he explained to Alf. 'And keep 'em hustlin'. Git a move on, *now!*'

Sullenly, with hanging heads, the line of men took up the trail. Egan accompanied Alf a short distance, giving him his instructions.

At that opening of the cutting season, the lumberjacks had not yet moved out to a permanent camp, but one was now under construction, and travoy roads were being run down to the water. All hands were to be put to work on the new camp, in order that it might be completed before the first fall of snow made it essential to begin the cutting.

'You keep 'em hustlin',' were Egan's last instructions, as he left Alf at the edge of the terrain.

'Step lively there!' called Alf. He glanced back as the line entered the woodland trail among the trees, and saw

Egan standing watching them, the humped shoulder distorting his form to grotesque proportions. A spasm of hatred and disgust ran through Alf as he looked back and saw him. Egan had been his evil star; he would have the reckoning with him someday. He ordered the men to step faster.

They proceeded up the bank of the river, along which some rough grading had already been done, and trees felled, to permit the passage of wagons and teams. As he walked along in the rear of the men, Alf looked about him in approval of the timber. There was a fine first growth of pine and red spruce, strong enough to have largely choked out the undergrowth of hazel and the spindling birch and poplar.

Surveying it in the light of his knowledge of timber values, Alf saw that there ought to be a clean, fat profit from these limits. He saw that Auguste Sorel was injuring his own interests, with the typical short-sightedness of the ex-peasant, in keeping his employees dissatisfied, and in a state of resentment against him. As for Egan, this much must certainly have been clear to him, but no doubt he was playing a deeper game.

At any rate, Alf knew enough of the lumber business to see that there should have been no difficulty in paying the men the standard wage.

For his own satisfaction merely he resolved, independently of his motives in signing up with the company, to do his work the best way he knew. He meant, too, to establish friendly relations with the men. With this end in view, he walked along the line, engaging them in conversation, first one man and then another. And quickly a change manifested itself in their attitude toward him.

They had known him as one of the thugs whom Sorel occasionally brought up to the camp for a short-lived span of activity and bullying; now, to their surprise, they discovered a man like themselves, speaking their own language, and understanding their work.

By the time they had reached their destination, their suspicions and resentment were already beginning to evaporate; and by the middle of the morning, they were prepared to accept Alf for what he professed to be.

About four miles up the river was the cleared space for the new camp. Trees had been felled and brush grubbed out, great piles of sawed beams were lying about under the trees, and travoy roads, three feet wide, radiated into the district which was to be cut over that winter. Rollways were in process of construction at the edge of the gorge, over which heaps of sand had been dumped for the construction of a cement dam to gather in the spring freshets and start the logs.

A cookhouse, a bunkhouse, and some smaller buildings were in the course of construction. The men worked energetically under the supervision of Pascal, who was the carpenter. Alf watched the men, occasionally entering into conversation with them, especially Pascal. He had an odd feeling of pity for this ponderous middle-aged man driven from his small farm to work for the company. Appreciable progress had been made with nailing the long boards into position by the time the sound of the mill whistle came faintly to their ears out of the distance.

At the sound of it, the lumberjacks threw down their hoards and knocked off work for their dinners at noon. Then Alf discovered that he had forgotten to bring any.

'Eh, monsieur, you have no dinner?' called Pascal, who was seated on the ground nearby, munching. 'Come, monsieur, share mine, for I have more than I can eat.'

He held out a thick sandwich of meat and bread, which Alf accepted, sitting down beside the old man. After a while Pascal turned to Alf and said:

'Monsieur, if you are to be our new foreman we shall work more gladly than before. But for those dogs of Papineaus and Monsieur Smith, no more than we can help. Monsieur, it was never believed such a day as this would come, when Monsieur Destry's lands would have become Auguste Sorel's. I remember when he was nothing but a *habitant*, like the rest of us, and hated, even then, for his usury. Yes, monsieur, and now he owns the land and makes slaves of us, and has driven Monsieur Philippe and Mademoiselle Camille over there.'

He jerked his arm toward the crest at the top of the road.

'You know, monsieur, the son and daughter of our master, old Monsieur Edouard,' continued Pascal, dropping his voice. 'Come, monsieur, and I will show you, if you like.'

Alf accompanied Pascal along the trail that emerged from the end of the wagon-road. There was a stiff climb uphill. Arriving at the summit, they looked down into a long narrow valley rimmed with forest-clad hills. Beneath them was a patch of cleared land upon which shacks were dotted, among them a more prosperous-looking but still plain and primitive cabin of logs.

'That is the home that Monsieur Philippe and Mademoiselle Camille have built, since Auguste Sorel seized this land and took their home away from them,' said Pascal, pointing. 'This is what we call the colony, monsieur, for in those cabins live many of those who have been driven from their lands after their houses were burned . . . Two horses!' he shouted suddenly. 'My two fine horses, burned in their stable by those animals, and my wife forced to flee in her nightdress, monsieur!'

'You mean to say they burned you out in the middle of the night?' asked Alf.

'Monsieur, it is true. I told them that I should not hesitate to shoot the first man who entered my pasture, and they knew that I would keep my word. So it was at night they came. Two fine horses, monsieur, such as you would not buy today for five hundred *piastres* apiece. They came to my call, and I had never used the lash on them.'

Alf looked away in embarrassment. In his mind he was attempting to discriminate between ruthlessness and bestiality. The necessity of choosing hit him hard.

He was still standing silently beside Pascal when he heard the creak of a wagon behind. The driver was bringing up a fresh load of sawn planks. He left it in the vehicle, unhitched his span of horses, and led them up the trail toward the summit of the elevation, where were patches of green grass on the denuded slope that ran down toward the river. At the sight of Alf, old Robitaille's face grew black as a thundercloud; in spite of his confidences of the day before, he regarded Alf as one of the thugs who had helped to burn out Chamberland.

Pascal went up to him as he was removing the bits from his horses' mouths and began talking to him. The two men, still engaged in conversation, came back to where Alf was standing, and Pascal laid a hand obsequiously upon Alf's sleeve. 'Monsieur,' he said, 'this is the driver Robitaille, my friend. Monsieur, his home was burned too. He, too, is forced to work for the company.'

'So I understand,' said Alf.

'Monsieur,' continued Pascal timidly, 'I know you are a good man, a man with a heart, a man like the *habitant*. Is there no way in which all this can be stopped? It is true that nearly all our homes are now destroyed, monsieur, but it is our lands of which I speak. It is easy to build a home

67

— only a little lumber is required for such homes as satisfy us, but there must be the zeal that comes from the possession of the soil. And Monsieur Sorel has all the forest; why should he grudge us the little clearings that we have made for ourselves?

'It is the love of the little pieces of land on which we have lived all our lives. We ourselves have driven back the forest and made our lands, monsieur. Now they will go back to forest again, and all the work of our lives is ended. Monsieur, if it could be made known in America, could it not be stopped? The Yankees are so rich, and they say that they are kind, and wish all men to be rich like themselves. And assuredly there is no one in Canada to help us, for Monsieur Philippe is helpless, and Mademoiselle Camille, though she has the heart and spirit, is only a woman.'

Robitaille intervened with some growling unintelligible comment, and Pascal listened, and then turned to Alf again.

'Yes, monsieur, and, as Robitaille says, there is a very bitter spirit among the men. They are not dogs, or beasts, that they should be driven into the forests; and there has been talk of returning fire for fire, monsieur, even if it means the end of their jobs. The *habitant* is long-suffering, but he is reckless when he is aroused.'

Alf shook his head impatiently, it was hard to be appealed to in that way. 'Why, I don't see how I can help you,' he answered. 'I'm just a hired man like you, and I have to do what I'm told.' He felt that his sympathies were being worked upon, and it aroused him to anger. 'No, I can't help you,' he said sharply. 'And it's time to get back to work,' he added, glancing at his watch, which indicated five minutes off one.

But he heard Pascal and Robitaille whispering together as they went back down the hill. 'He wishes to help us,' he heard Pascal saying. 'He is not like Smith and the Papineaus.'

A small commotion in the clearing attracted Alf's attention as he strode back in the wake of Pascal and the teamster. The men were sullenly preparing to resume their work. In the middle of the group stood Alphonse Papineau, engaged in a vicious harangue. His face darkened as Alf appeared.

'Eh, you Collet, so this is the way you keep the men at work!' he snarled. 'Monsieur Smith sent me to see what they were doing, and now he is coming himself. A fine story I shall have to tell him, eh, Collet?'

He was clenching his fists and scowling, and the lumberjacks, loitering near, perceiving that the issue between the two seemed joined, gradually pressed forward.

'Papineau, Mr. Smith put me in charge of this job, and I had no instructions that they were not to knock off for their dinner,' said Alf.

'Dinner? It's past one o'clock, and they're lying about here *smoking*,' yelled Alphonse. 'I guess the last camp you worked in was a lumberyard, Collet.'

'Anyway, I'm taking orders from him,' said Alf. He turned round. 'Get back to work, boys,' he said. 'Papineau, if you've come to join the gang, you can take your coat off and get busy.'

A roar of delighted laughter from the men greeted this.

'If you didn't come here to work, get out of here and don't interfere.'

A flood of oaths poured from Alphonse's lips. The men had gathered closely about them. There was, for them, more than the personal interest in the quarrel. Instinctively they had known that Alf was with them, though Alf hadn't known it himself. Alf symbolised their cause, by some intuitive process of their minds which had actually very little to base itself upon.

But suddenly the sound of approaching wheels was heard, and a galloping horse, drawing a rig, came plunging into the middle of the group and scattered it, and Egan leaped to the ground. He came quickly up. 'Hey, what's this?' he blustered.

'Why, Monsieur Smith, I came here like you told me,' answered Alphonse, 'and it's ten minutes past one, and I see these men lying under the trees and smoking, and Collet walking about on the hill instead of keeping them at work, like you told him.'

'Well, what you got to say to that,

71

Collet?' snarled Egan.

'That's a lie, Mr. Smith,' said Alf. 'And anyway, I took my orders from you, and not from him.'

Even as he looked into Egan's face, he realised that the scene had been staged so that Egan could show his power over him to the men. Egan put out one hand and gripped Alf's shoulder as in a vice. He swung Alf round.

'See here, you Collet, that line of talk doesn't go in this camp!' he shouted. 'I give the orders here, and what I say goes. You can take your choice, Collet,' he continued. 'You can git your day's pay and take a damn good hiding from me before you go, or you can git to work right now and do what Alphonse tells you. Which is it to be, Collet?' he continued, complacently glancing about him as he spoke.

All the men looked from Egan to Alf, and hung upon his answer.

Alf held himself in check. 'Why, I didn't mean no harm, Mr. Smith. Sure I'll do what he says,' he fawned.

Egan grinned, and Alphonse burst into

loud laughter. At Egan's gesture, the crowd dissolved. Egan released his clutch on Alf. 'I guess you got some *sense* in your head, young feller, after all,' he said.

'It's no use. He cannot help us. He is afraid, like all the rest of them,' Alf heard Pascal say to Robitaille as he followed them back toward the camp.

The driver stroked his grey beard and nodded mournfully.

7

Alf ate alone in the cookhouse that night. He was grateful for this solitude, and human enough to be glad not to have to face Egan and the Papineaus after his humiliation that afternoon. He saw now that Egan, having successfully staged the play, believed him to be entirely subservient. And in a way that furthered Alf's plans; still the situation was very hard to bear.

Alf fell asleep in considerable dejection. He was up early in the morning. As he left his shack, a woman next door smiled and nodded to him. He had made a hit with the lumberjacks, at any rate. Even the little cook's greeting in the cookhouse seemed warmer than before.

Egan and the Papineaus soon appeared on the scene. Egan grunted, and the Papineaus whispered and laughed as they looked at him. Alf noticed that each of them carried a stout stick with an iron heel, which he kept by his side. After the meal, Egan took down his belt from a nail and buckled it about him. The handle of a revolver showed in the holster. Egan turned to Alf.

'Say, you Collet, we're goin' on a little visit this mornin',' he said.

Alf saw that the little cook was scowling murderously.

The Papineaus rose, taking up their sticks, and hurriedly finishing devouring the flapjacks which they held clenched in their hands. Egan led the way toward the door.

The four were just about to leave the cookhouse when steps were heard outside, and Auguste Sorel looked in. There was an anticipatory smile upon his lined, cunning face. 'Well, boys, ready to settle up with Chamberland?' he inquired.

'Sure we're ready,' agreed old Aristide Papineau, displaying his yellow fangs; and his son, Alphonse, grinned too.

'Say, you betcha we don't fix him good!' said Egan with a grin. 'I hear Chamberland started repairin' his roof yesterday, after you gave him a week's notice to clear off the limits. I guess you don't stand for that, Sorel.'

'No, no,' Auguste said, smiling. 'But don't hurt him if you can help it, and don't treat him too rough. And be careful not to destroy his bed or any of his things, but particularly his bed. He'll want a nice, comfortable bed out in the forest.'

The grins grew wider. Sorel spoke in bitter irony in a fury of subdued malice. His glance fell upon Alf and Alf grinned too. He grinned from policy, and yet dirty as the business in hand was, something in him rejoiced at the suffering that was to be meted out to another. Some baser part of him was glad at the prospect of this manifestation of power.

Might was right. Alf had learned that in his own bitter apprenticeship. Let Chamberland, too, learn the meaning of injustice.

'No, be sure you don't hurt him,' said Sorel, smiling malignantly. 'That is the last of these squatters, isn't it, Mr. Smith?'

'Jest about,' answered Egan. 'I guess Mademoiselle Camille will find room for the Chamberland family in the colony. She and Monsieur Philippe are very hospitable.'

'The colony — yes, the colony,' said Sorel, smiling at some thought. 'Make a good job of it while you're about it, but don't hurt Chamberland or his old woman; I hear she has been sick. And remember about the bed. Come back soon and let me know how it went off. I shall be anxious to hear.'

He turned away, looking like an old wolf, and went toward the office. The Papineaus took up their iron-tipped sticks.

'Come on, Collet!' shouted Egan.

Alf accompanied the three across the tongue of land, Sorel turning to watch them as they passed the office. At the door of every hut a scowling woman was standing. Alf heard one of them mutter a curse. Egan heard it, and looked at her and laughed. All the lumberjacks' wives knew what the destination of the party was, and many of them had gone through the same experience that Chamberland and his wife were to undergo that morning. Alf loathed the business. He felt ashamed and humiliated, and glad to get away; at the same time he set himself defiantly to the undertaking, and choked down those feelings rising up in him.

They crossed the terrain, and, leaving the flat behind them, began to ascend a trail that ran across a projecting rocky ledge beyond the head of the lake. Then came a mile or two across a dense burned-over jungle of raspberry briers and blueberry shrubs.

Presently the waters of another smaller lake came into view. Situated near the head of this was a clearing of perhaps two acres in extent. It had the appearance of having been snatched with much labour from the forest, which was already beginning to throw out outposts of reclamation in the shape of small conifers and birch saplings, straggling in irregular lines toward the centre. Many of the stumps of the larger trees, too strongly rooted in the ground to be pulled, still remained, rotting in the soil, where they had stood for years. The lower edge of this pasture was waterlogged from the overflow of the little stream that ran down to feed the lake, and here and there a few thin sheep, a cow and a horse were grazing in the rank grass, which was everywhere overgrown with sheep-laurel.

Set into the centre of this clearing, Alf perceived another of the unpainted wretched shacks that seemed a feature of the country. It consisted of a single storey, built of weather-blackened timbers, and crazily open to the weather under the eaves. As the party descended the trail toward it, a woman appeared in the entrance, surveyed them for a moment under her extended hand, and then uttered a shrill cry.

The next moment a tall, bent old man had appeared behind her, flanked by two half-grown boys. As the four advanced across the pasture, old Chamberland stooped and reappeared in position with a long gun in his hands: the muzzle he presented at the breast of the nearest man. This was Alphonse Papineau, who promptly darted behind his father, who in turn fell back behind Egan.

'By God, I'll shoot the first man who

interferes with me!' shouted the old man in French, his features contorted in murderous hate.

Egan stepped forward. 'You've got to get out, Chamberland!' he called. 'That's the orders, and you can have just one hour to pack up and move. If you don't like it, you can see Mr. Sorel afterwards,' he added contemptuously.

The old man, with a furious gesture, covered Egan with his gun. Egan was no coward. Alf saw his hand drop to his holster. He knew that before Chamberland's finger pressed the trigger, Egan would have sent home his bullet, helpless though he appeared. But suddenly the old woman sprang between them and flung herself at Egan's knees.

'Listen, Monsieur Egan, only listen!' she pleaded. 'For fifty years we have lived here. Before you were born, we were living here. We built this home and cleared this forest. Always Monsieur Destry told us, 'You may stay and welcome, but if you take out a patent on your land, no one can ever turn you away after I die.' And one day my man goes to

80

Quebec to a lawyer, who says he will take out a patent for him for twenty dollars. My man gives him the twenty dollars, and we owned this land. Now Monsieur Sorel tells us no — '

Egan raised his hand with a scornful gesture. 'Forget it,' he retorted. 'Maybe your man did get swindled by one of those land lawyers, but that's an old story in these parts, and it doesn't go. You've got no patent on this land. The boss has had the land records looked up, and there's not one of you who's got a patent. You're just squatters, and you've got to go.'

The old woman sprang to her feet, clasping her hands before Alf in wild appeal. 'Monsieur, you will have pity on us and tell him not to destroy our home! Monsieur Sorel would not have the heart to turn us out after these fifty years. He does not want our house. He will not lumber here for a long time, and even when he does, how should we interfere with him. No, monsieur, he will not have the heart to turn us out into the forest, like wild beasts, at this time of the year, with winter coming, and us grown old, and the children — '

Alf shifted uneasily under her plea. He looked to Egan, who interposed brusquely. 'All that ain't got *nothing* to do with me,' he answered in surly English. 'I got my orders. Come, git a move on! You got jest one hour and no more!'

'*Mais qu'est-ce qu'il dit?*' demanded the old woman frantically of Alf. But Alf's gesture made a translation unnecessary. With a wild cry she ran back to her husband, who stood stock-still, aiming his gun at Egan's breast.

'If you take one step forward, *I shoot!*' he said with dreadful gravity.

Egan remained motionless. Only his eyes moved. They moved toward what Chamberland had failed to see in his agitation — toward Aristide and Alphonse Papineau, who had crept round to the rear door of the shack and were even now inside. Behind old Chamberland's head, Alf could see the wolfish fangs of Aristide.

Suddenly one of the boys started and cried. He clutched at his father's arm.

Chamberland swung about — too late. The iron heel of Aristide Papineau's stick crashed on his skull, knocking him senseless. The gun flew from his hand to Egan's feet. Egan picked it up.

With a scream, one of the boys sprang at Aristide, who gave him a kick in the stomach that doubled him, groaning, upon the floor. With that, the blood began to pound in Alf's ears. He took a step toward Aristide with clenched fists, and saw Aristide glance at him with suspicion and surprise. Alf stopped. He had been on the point of making a fool of himself. The next moment, Alphonse had called something to his father, and, leaving the old woman alternately sobbing and mumbling over the unconscious man and raising her arms in wild denunciation, Egan and the Papineaus began bundling out the wretched furniture. There was little except the table, chair, stove, and a dilapidated bed, and a heap of blankets in a little partitioned-off place in which the boys slept. In a few minutes these pieces, wrecked, and almost unrecognisable for what they had been, had been flung out into the pasture.

Dragging away the two boys, the men carried out old Chamberland, who was still unconscious, while his wife, her grey hair streaming about her shoulders, hobbled beside him, sending up her wild appeals to the sky. Some kerosene was found in a tin can. Some of the rags from the boys' bed were drenched with it. Egan applied the match. Almost in an instant the fifty-year-old timbers, rotten and bone dry, flared up in a great blaze. A volume of greasy smoke came pouring out of the cabin.

At the sight of the conflagration, the old woman flung herself on Alphonse like a demoniac, screeching and clawing at him. Alphonse, laughing bestially, dealing her a blow that stretched her upon the ground.

Something broke in Alf at that. He thought of his own mother, the pretty mother whom he had worshipped who was still a sort of ideal, something that had always strengthened him in times of stress and temptation. The next moment,

Alf had darted forward and dealt Alphonse a blow in the face that sent him staggering backward. He tripped over the projecting root of a tree and went sprawling heavily upon the ground.

Alphonse picked himself up slowly, staring at Alf in stupefied amazement. Alf squared up to him as he rose. '*That* won't go here!' he shouted.

'No?' sneered Alphonse, and with a crafty movement he came sidling up to Alf. 'Mebbe you tell me what you mean by that, knocking me down?' he drawled in English.

There was a shifty movement of his right arm. Alf caught the glimpse of a knife-blade between the fingers. He stood there for a moment, in a poised tension. Just as instinctively, Alf waited him, his fists in fighting position, ready for the other's move. Alf knew the time for a show-down with Alphonse Papineau had come. He had no fear of his knife. He had served his apprenticeship in many a lumber-camp fight, and a jagged scar along his left forearm attested to his initiation. He knew that fists were better than knives any day, and he knew that he could get his blow in first. A man with a knife in his hand is bound by the contemplated blow, his mind is on his weapon; fists are free.

But Egan stepped between them, his face dark with rage. 'Nix on that stuff! Put 'er back, Alphonse!' he commanded.

Alphonse was sullenly replacing the knife in the sheath at his belt when there came a clattering of hoofs along the trail, and a moment later a young woman riding a bay horse came cantering across the pasture toward them.

8

She was dark and slender and not very tall, and she sat astride her horse with a supple boyish grace, swinging to each of its movements with the freedom of one habituated to the saddle. But this saddle was a thing of tatters, disgorging stuffing through rips and tears. The woman's dress was in keeping with it, for it was faded and old; and there was a faded sunbonnet on her head, beneath which her hair, unloosed by her gallop, tumbled about her shoulders. Still she came on, with a furious urging of her heels against the flanks of the bay.

With a gesture of indescribable scorn, she pulled in the horse, and, dismounting, kneeled down at the side of old Chamberland and his wife. Chamberland was slowly coming back to consciousness. He dragged himself a little distance back from the burning shack, and, sitting up on the ground, shook his fist while the blood from the scalp wound streamed down his face. He shouted wildly, waving his arms. Aristide and Alphonse shouted back, mocking taunts at him. The old woman fondled the injured boy, crooning over him as she sat on the ground.

The hut was now a pillar of fire, sending up a column of dense greasy smoke that streamed across the sky. The heat drove the raiders farther away. Old Chamberland was still shouting, and the Papineaus pointed toward the lake and made derisive signs indicative of putting out the flames with water.

'Well, I guess this nest will need some rebuilding,' Egan soliloquised. 'Come, boys, let's git out of here.'

But the woman had mounted her horse again and ridden past them, and now reined in and barred the way. She was fury personified. Standing up in her stirrups, she pointed the little quirt she carried at the three men, and broke into a torrent of denunciation.

Alf could not at first follow the swift, excited flow of language, but her gestures were unmistakable. Under her denunciations, the two Papineaus looked down and shifted their feet sullenly. Egan, however, eyed the woman with a stare of insolent admiration.

'Now, Miss Camille, it ain't these men's fault nor mine,' he said. 'It's Mr. Sorel's orders and what he says goes.'

'You're lying to me, Mr. Smith. You are a partner here, and everybody knows it is at your instigation that Monsieur Sorel permits this wickedness. Why should he wish to injure his own people? And your men have nearly killed that old man and the boy, and struck the old woman in the face.'

Egan grinned. He had never taken his eyes from the woman's face and throat. She swung upon the Papineaus.

'And as for *you*,' she cried, 'what do you call yourselves? *Men?* Men, to strike down an old man and woman and a boy? Men, to set fire to two old people's homes and drive them into the forest at this season of the year? And they *Canayens* like yourselves. Men? That isn't men's work. That's wolves' work — no, no wolf or any other beast would descend to that level. A man would throw up that sort of job and go out to earn an honest livelihood.'

'Now see here, Miss Camille,' interposed Egan. 'This is the company's land, and them squatters have got no business on it. We give 'em fair notice to quit, and they wouldn't take it. And all this talk can't alter that.'

'The *company's land?*' cried the woman addressed as Camille. 'It was my *father's land*, and he never sold it. He told me before he left that he was only planning to mortgage it. And if he did sell it, who got the money? Auguste Sorel and you, and someday there shall be an accounting.' She turned upon the Papineaus once more. 'As for *you*,' she cried, 'wolves don't eat wolves. Who do you think will ever speak to you, eat with you, shake you by the hand in all of Canada, you pair of Judases?'

Aristide's two yellow fangs disclosed themselves as he snarled an unintelligible answer. Camille's vehemence had momentarily cowed both father and son; perhaps, too, they felt something of the old servile fear of the daughter of their seigneur. They broke into hoarse cries, baying her, shaking with rage, but cringing under her contempt.

But suddenly Alphonse shouted a vile word at her, and swiftly Camille raised her quirt and brought the pliant tip down on his shoulders, and again across his face. A spurt of blood flew from Alphonse's lip. He started back, and then ran at her with a malediction, seizing the rearing animal by the reins, and snatching the whip out of her hand. He raised it, mad with fury, his face twisted into the semblance of an obscene gargoyle.

Alf always afterward remembered the scornful look on Camille's face as she sat her rearing horse without flinching, waiting to receive Alphonse's blow. And this time he would have intervened with more decision than before, but Egan anticipated him. Before the blow fell, Egan had snatched the whip out of Alphonse's hand and dealt him a blow that stretched him senseless upon the ground. And if Alphonse's face had been ferocious, Egan's was at that moment bestial, and the look he shot at Camille chilled Alf to the marrow, embodying, as it did, an awful blending of hate and lust, a combination possible only to the most degraded.

Alf stepped quickly to the side of Camille's horse. 'Please go,' he said quietly.

But, wholly unmoved by this fracas, she turned her scorn on Alf in turn. 'What, another Yankee?' she said in those tones of mordant mockery. 'Another Yankee come to help burn our people out of their homes and drive them into the woods among the beasts? A fit employment, monsieur, just fit for one of your people. For you see, thank God, there are no more Papineaus in this country.'

Alphonse was getting up with a bewildered air. Aristide was scowling at Egan. Alf stood by helplessly. For a moment Camille hesitated, and then rode back to the Chamberland group and dismounted by them again.

'I guess you kinda forgot where you got off, Alphonse,' said Egan. 'And you too, Collet. Come on, boys, let's git a move on. This job's through, anyway.' He drew his sleeve across his damp forehead, and, after hesitating a moment, Alphonse joined his father, and the four took up the trail again, Egan leading, and the two Papineaus following, occasionally glancing back at Alf, who brought up the rear.

It was for Alf, not Egan, that Alphonse reserved his blackest scowls. Alf let himself fall well behind them, and as he strode along, he cursed himself for his folly which had made the sight of a woman struck something unbearable. He would have to school himself better if he did not mean to give away his game.

He had recognised Camille's breeding immediately, in spite of her ragged dress, and he had hated her as a representative of that world which he hoped someday to conquer. He had tried to help, and had brought down a tongue-lashing on himself in turn. He must do better than that.

He caught up with the party when it was nearing the office. Auguste Sorel was talking to Dubois, the little storekeeper, upon the stoop when they arrived. He descended to meet them, his china-blue eyes scanning their faces keenly.

'Well, so you fixed Chamberland, *hein?*' he demanded of Egan.

'Sure we fixed him.' Egan grinned. 'Burned his shack to blazes. The old boy tried to git gay with his gun, though, and Aristide here had to bean him.'

Sorel shook his head and rolled up his eyes in mock solicitude. 'That is unfortunate,' he answered unctuously. 'It goes to my heart to see these unhappy people suffer from their own folly and willfulness.'

The Papineaus burst into laughter.

'And that damn Destry woman came ridin' up and butted in,' said Egan.

'You mean Mademoiselle Destry?' Sorel had turned on him with a sudden snarl. It was as if the ingrained deference of the peasant toward his lord had suddenly come out in him; he would fight Camille Destry, but he would not hear her misspoken.

And there was something more to it than that. Alf, watching the pair, saw the concealed, latent, murderous hostility that

Sorel felt toward Egan blaze out in him. He had never seen so much concentrated, concealed malignity, and he knew that Egan, shrewd as he was, and whatever his hold over Sorel, did not suspect it. It gave him a clue to Sorel's own hints and approaches to him. Alf felt that he had another thread in his hands.

'Sure, that's who I mean,' answered Egan, quite unruffled. 'She come ridin' up on that bay of hers and started raisin' hell with Alphonse and Aristide. Say, you ought to have heard the things she said to 'em. And she said we didn't own the limits, and there'd have to be an accountin',' he added maliciously.

Sorel glowered at him; Egan had got home here. 'Yes, yes, it is unfortunate, very unfortunate, all this ill feeling,' he said dryly.

'Well, I guess Chamberland's about the last of them squatters,' said Egan.

'Yes, yes,' answered Sorel. 'You did not hurt the Chamberlands' bed, I hope? It is a good thing all this business is ended, and no doubt Mademoiselle Camille and Monsieur Philippe will accommodate the

Chamberlands on their own property. Come into the office, Smith, I wish to speak to you.'

Sorel put his hand on Egan's shoulder and drew him inside. The action seemed a singular one to Alf. Egan seemed to flow under Sorel's hand, as if his bulking body dissolved at the touch of the keener mind. Alf knew at that moment which side he would elect to serve, if matters came to the point of choosing.

The door closed behind them. Standing outside, Alf saw the Papineaus looking at him and whispering together. They glared at him in bitter hate, though it was Egan, not he, who had given Alphonse that blackening eye, and Camille, not he, who had puffed that bloody lip. For a moment, it looked as if Alphonse meant to bring his quarrel with Alf to a settlement there and then. But Aristide took his son by the arm and whispered something, which was received with an outburst of vicious laughter; and, after an insolent, challenging look which Alf ignored, Alphonse permitted his father to lead him away in the direction of the bunkhouse.

Alf lingered irresolutely on the terrain till Egan came out of the office. He went straight up to him, took him by the arm, and drew him some distance away. Then he put his hand on his shoulder in that fashion Alf resented so much, and spun him insolently round.

'Say, you, Collet, what kind of a game are you tryin' to pull?' he asked.

'Why, I wasn't trying any game, Mr. Smith,' answered Alf.

'Yestidday you made trouble between Alphonse and the men, and today you struck him. I don't quite get you,' said Egan, surveying him with cool insolence. 'Nope, I don't quite get you, because after that talk you and me had the other night I nat'rally thought you saw how the land lay. Well, there ain't no middle ground fer you, my lad, and it's one thing or the other. Are you and me in together like I was sayin', or ain't we? Because, if we ain't, you c'n beat it out of this camp as quick as you know how.'

It was the insolence of the old ward bully, for whom Alf had rotted in the pen.

97

For a moment he had the single instinct to grapple with the man, maul him and tear him, and force the truth from his lips. But he kept himself in rein. 'Sure I'm in with you, Mr. Smith,' he answered, letting his eyes fall.

Egan stared at him with satisfied malignity. He felt quite sure of him now. 'Then you and me'll have a little talk together by-and-by, Collet,' he said.

9

It was the next Sunday that the talk developed. Most of the men had gone over to Dupont's, a shebeen three miles away, to drink, a custom which Egan encouraged as riveting the fetters of debt more firmly on the workers. Egan came into Alf's shack and eyed him as one sums up a fool.

'I guess you've sorta started in wrong, Collet,' he said. 'You wasn't called upon to hit Alphonse. I do all the hittin' that's needed in this camp. Them Frenchies take it from me, but if I hadn't stopped Alphonse usin' that knife on you I guess there wouldn't be much left of you. 'Nother thing, Aristide was sayin' you looked at him kinda queer when we was burnin' out Chamberland.'

'Why,' stammered Alf, 'it seemed kind of raw seeing Alphonse knock down that old woman.'

'Shucks!' retorted Egan. 'You'll soon git

used to that kind of thing, Collet. It ain't as if them Frenchies was real folks like you and me. Why, they ain't nothin' but animals. And as fer burnin' 'em out — why, that ain't nothin' to them! Them crazy shacks is always catchin' fire. They jest go and squat somewheres else. And that Camille and her brother Philippe, they take 'em all in.' He put his hand on Alf's shoulder. 'If you ain't the damnedest fool in the world, you got velvet, jest plain velvet ahead of you. Why, money's the easiest thing in the world to git, if you know how to set about gittin' it. A man who works fer a lumberjack's wages is jest a plain sucker, Collet, that's all there is to say about that.' He paused reflectively and eyed Alf with that touch of old suspicion for a moment. 'Set down; I'm goin' to talk straight to you now, Collet.'

Alf obeyed, and Egan seated himself opposite him.

'Remember what I was tellin' you about Sorel & Smith bein' me?' he asked.

Alf nodded assent.

'The time's jest about ripe,' Egan meditated, 'fer the Smith part to put the

Sorel part on the scrapheap. I got Sorel where I want him, and he knows it. Mebbe I was wrong to put the old man wise the way I did that mornin' to what that gel Camille said about an accountin' fer these lands, but that got his goat, sure enough, and it's started somethin'. Sorel's scared stiff, because there was plenty of crooked work, not about that deal but about what went before it.

'Ya see, Collet, these lands belonged to old Destry, and Sorel had been cheatin' him fer years as his agent. Sorel took him down to the U.S. to make a deal over the lands, he himself, unknown to Destry, bein' the purchaser, and not the person who was actin' fer him. Now there's a whole raft of papers Sorel's got in the safe in his house, which would show up all them deals he done with Destry's money if any interested parties, like Camille, fer instance, was to git hold of 'em.

'Sorel don't dare destroy them, because he knows the time might come when he'd have to produce 'em, and he ain't got the brains to falsify 'em, and he don't dare tell nobody about it and ask him to. He's jest been puttin' things off, I guess, but now he's plannin' to take them papers to Montreal and put 'em in some place where nobody can't git at 'em.'

The strange look of meditation on Egan's face fascinated Alf. Egan considered Alf plastic material in his hands; he had disarmed himself.

'I guess I done pretty well by meself, Collet, by usin' what brains I had,' Egan continued. 'I started life no better 'n you, in a slum in Fall City. Drunken father and stepmother . . . I clouted her over the head one day and left her lyin' senseless in a corner. Beat it, sold newspapers in the streets, then got into the ring. Then I went into politics. But I wasn't satisfied. I'd got dreams, Collet, dreams of gettin' out of it and bein' a little boss on my own somewheres in the country.

'And then my chance come — here. I got wise to this game Sorel was playin' with Destry when they was in the United States, and I got Sorel in my pocket. Sorel's game's to be what Destry useter be, but — ' He leaned forward impressively. ' — that's what *I'm* goin' to be,

Collet. And the man that's got the lands and Destry's gel has got the job Destry had. That's what I'm playin' fer, Collet, and I don't mind lettin' you know, because the game's as good as won now, and there won't be nothin' left of Sorel when I git through with him. But there's one thing I gotta have.' His arm shot out again, his fingers gripped Alf's shoulder, his face was thrust forward almost into Alf's. 'I want them papers Sorel's got in his safe, Collet. Ya see, soon as I can prove Sorel swindled old Destry, the lands go back to that gel Camille to make up fer the money he stole. Sorel has to hand 'em back to avoid goin' to jail. And them papers shows jest what game Sorel was playin' with Destry all them years. I seen 'em once, but I couldn't put my hands on 'em then. Now the time's come fer me and Ma'mzelle Camille to fix things up, and nat'rally we'll want the lands, and we won't have no more use fer Sorel. You git me, Collet?'

'Yes,' answered Alf, swallowing hard. 'I — I get you, Mr. Smith.' But somehow the thought of Camille as Egan's wife struck him as something monstrous. He was amazed at the feeling of blind resentment surging up in him.

'Well?' There was a sinister flicker in Egan's eyes. 'Well, Collet? I guess you don't git me after all. As I was sayin', Sorel's got them papers in a safe in his house. It's in the little room at the back, and he sleeps in the big room in the front, on the floor above. There ain't no one else in the house nights, because the old woman who looks after him comes every day from the shacks and goes home again when her work's done. Them papers would go easy into a small suitcase, I guess. I got a dispatch case'd be about big enough. Nat'rally Sorel and Destry didn't carry on a big correspondence with letter files to hold it. We c'n sort the papers out afterward. And then it'll be velvet, *velvet*, boy.

'Yep, the time's about ripe, Collet. I've let that old fool, Sorel, make enemies of the folks round here by his burnings till they're ripe to murder him. They won't be sorry to see him go. And I guess they'll be glad to see the new brooms, meanin' me and Camille. And you, foreman. And them Papineaus gits straight to hell. I guess you're wise now, Collet.'

Alf swallowed hard. He put on the most innocent expression of which he was capable. 'You mean you — you want *me* to get those papers out of Sorel's safe?' he asked.

'Sure *that's* what I mean,' sniggered Egan. 'That's what I mean, and *that's* what you're goin' to *do*, Collet. Didn't you tell me you was wanted fer a puffin' job in the U.S.? I'd do it meself, only I ain't no crook, and I never done nothin' like that. But you won't have no trouble. Why, a job like this is velvet, compared to what you've done over there, hey, Collet? Because I ain't no damn fool, Collet, and I guess it's more than one job you're wanted fer, hey, Collet?

'No, you won't have no trouble, and when Sorel finds out his safe's busted, he'll be too busy listenin' to what I'm tellin' him to wonder if it was you done it or no. So we'll git down to business. I got the soup, and I got everything you'll want — a flash, a bit and brace, cold chisel, jimmy, and keys. I got it all from a crook I useter know, jest fer this. Why, with the kind of safe Sorel's got, it'll be like openin' a kid's money-box.'

Alf knew too well exactly what was required of him. 'Puffing' was a method used on antiquated safes of the kind Sorel was likely to possess. Instead of the door being blown off, a little 'soup' was poured through a small opening drilled into the combination box, and the ensuing explosion, when properly muffled, was hardly louder than the detonation of a small revolver. The box being shattered, it was a simple matter to manipulate the levers with a pair of pliers and open the door.

It was not so much the suggestion of the crime that disgusted Alf as the realisation that Egan was planning to use him as a tool again, as he had used him before. A flame of rage burned in him as he looked into Egan's face opposite his own. 'You go to hell,' said Alf with deliberate emphasis. He could have cursed himself the next moment. But Egan only grinned.

'Say, you ain't thinkin' right,' he

answered. 'You think agen, Collet, and mebbe you'll see it in a different light. How d'you suppose you're goin' to git away from this camp, bein' wanted in the U.S. as you are, if I was to tip off the dicks? There ain't no way outta here except through St. Joseph, and you'd be pinched the minute you stepped into the depot at Montreal. Didn't think of that I guess, did you, Collet?'

Alf played his game now with all his power. 'You — you don't mean you — you'll have me pinched if I don't agree to do what you said, Mr. Egan?' he asked.

'That's exactly what I do mean,' answered Egan, grinning.

Then Alf flung himself into his role to avoid the only possible alternative, which was to smash Egan's face in. 'Say, gimme a chance, Mr. Smith!' he pleaded. 'I ain't no crook — honest I ain't. I don't wanta get mixed up with no dirty job like that. I come up here to run straight,' he whined.

Egan stood up and put his pincer-like hands on Alf's shoulders. Again he thrust his face into his, jaw out and working. 'See here, young feller,' he shouted, 'I

107

mean jest what I say. You're goin' to puff that safe tonight, and you're goin' to git them papers, and you and me's goin' to work hand in hand together, meanin' you're goin' to do what I tell you. And if you don't like that, you c'n go into the pen as soon as the dicks have fixed up your extradition papers. And mebbe they're wanting you fer somethin' more than jest blowin' a safe, hey, Collet?'

The shrewd thrust made Alf wince. He was thinking with the utmost rapidity all the while Egan talked. He was determined not to obey, if only because he knew Sorel was more than a match for Egan. He had not summed up Sorel as lightly as Egan had done. He had definitely decided that Sorel would prove the master of the situation. But he must temporise, to gain time to think things over.

'Say, Mr. Smith, it's kind of sudden, the way you sprung it on me,' Alf faltered with a dreary smile. 'I wasn't expecting it somehow.'

'Yep, I'm quick, Collet. That's my way,' answered Egan complacently, as he saw

Alf was on the point of yielding.

'Say, will you gimme a little time to think it over?'

'Sure, take all the time you want, Collet,' answered Egan, moving toward the door, 'so long as you let me know by night. You c'n set there all day thinkin' if you want to, but I guess you'll come round, unless you got a kinda hankerin' after the pen. And don't you be a damn fool,' he continued, turning on Alf with sudden ferocity. 'Mebbe I did spring it quick on you, but, Lord, don't you see where your own interest lies. It ain't as if I was askin' you to steal. It ain't nothin' but gettin' back some papers from a crook and showin' him up, the same as any crook might do. All you got to do is to puff that safe of Sorel's and bring me the papers, and I'll kick the old fool off these limits tomorrow.'

'Say!' called Alf, arrested by a sudden thought, as Egan put his hand upon the door. 'What happened to Destry after he went down to the U.S. and fixed up that deal with Sorel? Had a stroke or something, didn't he?'

Egan's grin grew very broad. 'Why, that's the tale we give out among the folks up here,' he answered. 'Only Sorel and Camille and that brother of hers knows jest what happened. But I'll tell you, Collet. Destry got croaked in Fall City the same night he made his deal with Sorel. Guess some thug knew the old guy was carryin' a wad around with him and followed him. Hit on the head and had his skull stove in, and nobody identified him fer months till they dug up his body to identify him.'

And Alf, staring after Egan as he swaggered away, felt something like horror begin to stir in him as he understood who the dead man had been.

10

It might have been coincidence, it might have been another man, but Alf knew it was neither. He knew Destry was the man whom he had seen lying dead in the slum gutter. Destry was the man for whose murder he had slaved in the pen; Sorel and Egan had conspired his death, and this was the clue to Egan's partnership in the company. And it was this crime that linked the pair together and threw a totally different light upon the situation.

For ten wild seconds Alf stood in horror inside the shack. Then suddenly a wilder exultation filled him. Things were coming his way; how, he could not foresee. But here were all the ingredients necessary for his compounding; he need never look further. Before Egan had gone ten paces from the shack Alf was at his side.

'I guess I'll go, Mr. Smith,' he said.

'Sure you'll go,' snickered Egan.

'Didn't take you so long to find it out, did it?'

It was a little after midnight when Alf found himself outside Sorel's house. The long log building of two stories was set among the trees on the hillside, overlooking the mill. A promenade around it showed that the ground floor contained three rooms, the little one at the back of which Egan had spoken being a small extension used as an office.

It was the work of only a few moments to pry back the window catch and enter. Alf stood inside, turning his flash slowly about the room. It was very plainly furnished — a table, a large desk, two chairs, and a *habitant* rag rug upon the floor were about all it contained, except a pair of caribou horns on a wall, and the safe, set in a recess a foot above the ground.

A single glance at this showed Alf that it was one of an ancient kind, impressively strong to the uninitiated, and discouraging to local burglary talent, but a joke to the city cracksman. It was even to Alf a joke, though his own knowledge of cracksmanship was more or less a theoretical one, except for that single expedition on which Murphy had taken him.

However, he understood what was to be done. Before starting, he satisfied his latent sixth sense as to the absence of any danger. The whole house was dark and perfectly silent. The night was dark; there was an hour before the moon rose. Alf opened the door of the room and stood listening. When one listens in a house of sleepers, even of a single sleeper, gradually the personality of the sleeping person seems to project itself toward the listener. One seems to hear the breathing, one becomes almost conscious of the vital processes through intervening doors and walls. But Alf, listening at the door, heard nothing, derived no consciousness of Sorel's proximity. And slowly the feeling was borne in upon him that the house was empty. If Sorel had been asleep upstairs, he would have known it.

He had no time to waste speculating on this point, however. Satisfied that he was not likely to be molested, he closed the door, and turned to the safe. The little bead-torch flashed a thread of white light upon the combination box. Kneeling down, Alf started to drill the hole to hold the soup. Patiently he worked, and for a long time the metal seemed to be invulnerable; then, bit by bit, the point of the drill began to bite its way into the steel. At last Alf stepped back. Taking up the rag rug, he wrapped it about the safe to muffle the sound of the explosion. He placed the detonant in the hole that he had cut. He lit the tiny fuse. He stepped back.

In a few moments a dull crack, like the sound of a dulled pistol discharge, followed, accompanied by the tumbling click of the disarranged mechanism within. Alf removed the rug, and with that curious impulse toward orderliness, which stamped him at once as temperamentally un-adapted for a life of crime, he replaced it in its former position on the floor. He looked at the safe. It appeared intact; only a close inspection showed what had occurred.

Drawing a little pair of pliers from his

pocket, Alf quickly manipulated the clutches and pulled back the levers. The door of the safe swung open. Inside were a number of ledgers and other books of accounts, but a quick examination of these by the light of his torch showed Alf that they had reference to the affairs of the company during the four years of its existence. Alf opened the single deep drawer. Inside was a bundle of papers, and a small book marked 'Les Affaires de M. Destry.'

Alf stuffed the book and papers into the little dispatch case with which Egan had supplied him. He closed the door of the safe and stood up.

At the same moment he heard a click. A finger of light shone through beneath the door. Someone had turned on the electric light in the hall.

The door opened, and Camille Destry came into the room.

Their eyes met, and she choked back an exclamation. She put her hand to her breast with a quick convulsive movement. Though the safe appeared intact, Alf's attitude revealed everything.

115

She took a quick step toward him. 'You — who are you? What do you want? Why are you here?' she whispered.

Alf's eyes wandered from her to the window. He was speculating on the possibility suddenly leap. Or should he face her? It was a difficult moment of choice. His mind was not made up when a heavy footstep sounded in the passage.

Then, just as he was about to leap, a message in Camille's eyes arrested him. She made an imperative movement of her hand toward the corner behind the safe, which was blocked from observation by the large chair that was thrust forward there.

Only a moment longer Alf hesitated. Then, as quick as conscious thought may travel, he realised that Camille Destry's interests did not lie in betraying him; that this woman was as vitally concerned with the contents of Sorel's safe as he was. Immediately he stepped behind it and crouched down, just as Sorel crossed the threshold into the room.

He uttered an exclamation as he saw Camille. He switched on the light, which

116

filled the little room with a bright glare. Alf saw how Camille contrived to take up a position with her back to him, which both concealed him and hindered Sorel from advancing near enough to discover him. He could not see the safe from where he was, but he saw the thin edging between it and the door, which he had failed to close completely. Had Camille seen? Would Sorel see? Sorel was now advancing in to the middle of the room. But Camille did not move, and he stopped two or three feet from her.

'Well, monsieur!' Her voice was like ice. 'You told me that you would see me, and, finding the front door unlocked, I walked in. I waited for you here.'

'What do you wish to say to me, mademoiselle?' asked Sorel heavily.

'You know!' she burst out vehemently. 'You know, monsieur! How can you ask me that question? And how can you dare do such things to our own people, those whom you knew when you were a boy? What wrong have they done to you? Yes, I know what you would say, if you dared to speak the truth, that it is Smith, the man

Smith, who thinks by such means to force me into a marriage with him. Why, he does not understand us at all, if he thinks we are to be intimidated like that! It is you who understand so well . . .

'No, no, you are going to listen to me, because it was not easy for me to come to you, and it is not easy for me to speak to you calmly, and I shall not come here again. I believe that you have unjustly acquired my father's lands. It was not his purpose to sell them when he accompanied you over the border. I believe that Smith knows that, and has a hold over you on account of it. Spare me your denials, Monsieur Sorel!'

Sorel was breathing heavily. His face looked ghastly in the electric light.

'Well, monsieur, listen to what I have come to say to you. If you bought these lands, where is the money gone?'

'Mademoiselle, you do not understand that your father was heavily in debt. Nearly all the money was paid out to his creditors, as was his wish. If you insist the accounts shall be placed before you — '

' 'Nearly all?' But what of the rest?'

118

'How do I know, mademoiselle? When your father was murdered, who shall say how much money he had about him? One thousand? Ten thousand? Only the man who killed him knows.'

If Sorel's face was ghastly, Camille's was no less pale. Instead of accusing, she in turn began to shrink back before Sorel, almost as if she herself possessed the knowledge of some guilty secret.

'How can I give an accounting, then, mademoiselle?' Sorel pursued.

'Listen, monsieur,' said Camille with a sudden resolution. 'You have coveted my father's lands all your life. Never mind how you came by them. You have them. Keep them. I shall never intervene, I shall never seek an accounting, if — if you will restore our people to their little farms, where they do you no harm, and send this man Smith back to his own country. I will sign anything you please, do anything you ask — well what, monsieur, what do you say to that?'

Sorel said nothing for a while. He stood there, a chunky pillar of a man, one clenched fist upon the table seeming to support the whole weight of his body. Alf knew what thoughts were running through his mind. It was the blood guilt. The murder of Destry had linked Sorel and Egan inextricably.

'All this is untrue, mademoiselle,' said Sorel at length. 'As I have told you, these lands were fairly obtained by purchase; and as for the settlers, they were all warned to leave because they interfered with the lumbering.'

'Ah, so you must lie to me!' cried Camille impatiently. 'I have known you since my first recollections, Auguste Sorel, and you have always been the diplomatist. Is my offer not good enough for you? Think! The lands are yours forever. The people will gradually cease to hate you, and they will ascribe all that they have suffered to the man Smith, when he is gone. An honourable position, monsieur, all that you have ever wished for . . . is it not worth your while?'

'Mademoiselle, you persist in misjudging me.'

'If you refuse, I shall fight you. These wrongs cannot go on. Philippe and I have sown land to feed these people, and there is not grain enough to carry them through this winter. They are desperate. Smith is playing with you, but you are playing with fire. Will you agree?'

There was nothing of the bitter buffoon in Sorel now. His voice rumbled shakily through the room. 'No, it is impossible — what you propose — ' he stammered.

'Ah, you are tied hand and foot to this Smith, then, by other wrongs!'

'A thousand curses on him!' shouted Sorel, with sudden explosive fury. 'May he rot in his grave before you suffer wrong at his hands! You are the daughter of Monsieur Edouard. He shall not force you to be his wife.'

'He will never force me,' said Camille quietly.

Sorel checked himself as suddenly as he had begun. 'But what you propose is impossible, mademoiselle. I — I am not so bad as you think I am. I — your father was my master . . . No, no!' he shouted, seeming to regain his old attitude by a convulsive effort of will. 'I cannot work with you. We must remain enemies.'

'Very well, monsieur,' answered Camille coldly. She turned toward the door, and Sorel accompanied her out of the room, along the hall. Alf heard his voice drop to a whining protest.

The moment they were gone — Camille had pulled to the door — Alf was at the window, had raised the sash noiselessly, and made his exit with the dispatch case. He plunged into the tangles of frosted undergrowth along the mountain side, running on until he reached a little open place far from the house. The moon was beginning to rise, but its light was still dim. By the light of the torch Alf went quickly through the papers. Many of these had reference to Destry, and all such, as well as those with Destry's signature scrawled on them Alf put in his shirt. The rest he put back into the case.

At last he rose and looked about him. He found that the track which he had taken had brought him near the new wagon-road. He struck it after a little while, and started back along it in the direction of the camp.

The moon was now riding higher, its

light lay in bright pools along the way, cut off and intersected by the shadows of the branches. Out of this brightness, presently Alf saw a figure coming toward him. It was that of Camille. She stopped in front of him.

'I waited for you and searched for you. Never mind that, monsieur. Those papers from the safe. Not the money — that is yours, whatever you found. The papers — ' There was the pretence of conviction that he had found the papers, there was anxiety in her tone, there was contempt. Above all there was insistence. 'Those papers!' Suddenly her eyes fell upon the little dispatch case. 'Ah — h!' she breathed. 'In that case, if you please, monsieur.'

'Listen, mademoiselle!'

'No, no, I will not be put off with words. I protected you. Now you will give me those papers — not the money, but the papers, which mean nothing to you.'

'Mademoiselle, if you will let me explain — '

'Those papers!' She put her hand on the dispatch case. Alf saw that her agitation was becoming uncontrollable. 'Come, hand them over to me at once!'

'These are not yours. You don't understand. I want to tell you — '

But suddenly she flew at him like a fury. She tried to wrest the case from him. She panted in a mad wrestle with him. She would not listen to him. Alf had to tear the dispatch case forcibly from her and ran at full speed down the road toward the camp. He burst into his shack breathless.

Egan was lying there on the bed, waiting for him. He sat up, smiling sardonically, his deformed shoulder making a hideous hump of shadow against the wall by the light of the candle flame. 'Well, Collet?' he jeered.

Alf tossed the dispatch case upon the bed. 'I got 'em Mr. Smith,' he said. 'They're all in there. I couldn't stop to look at them, so I took all there was.'

'Good boy!' Egan grinned, picking up the case and getting upon his feet. 'Old Sorel didn't git wise?'

'No, he didn't wake up.'

'You done well, Collet,' said Egan

condescendingly, 'and I won't fergit it.' He swaggered out of the shack with the dispatch case.

Alf waited till he had crossed the terrain. Then by the light of the candle, he began poring once more over the papers that he had taken. He went through the book too. The whole appeared to be a complete disclosure of all of Destry's financial transactions with Sorel during a long period of years. If evidence of fraud existed, it was there.

At last Alf got up. Wrapping the book and papers in a neck-cloth, he raised one of the loose boards in the floor of the shack and placed them underneath it.

11

Egan came to Alf the next morning, and from the complacence of his countenance Alf gathered that he had not yet gone through the papers which Alf had given him; indeed, it was probable enough that Egan's mentality would not for some time enable him to digest them sufficiently to discover that they contained not a scrap of evidence that would incriminate Sorel.

'Say, Collet,' Egan began ingratiatingly, 'that was a fine bit of work you done last night. And now I'm goin' to send you out with the gang. And I ain't goin' to put you in charge of them neither. You'll work under the Papineaus. But I've talked to Alphonse and Aristide, and I've told 'em I won't stand fer no rough-house, so you won't have no trouble there.

'Ya see, it's this way, Collet. Jest as soon's I spring the game on Sorel, which might not be fer a day or two, you'll git what you got comin' to you. But till then we got to keep the Papineaus from guessin' that you and me's workin' together. So you'll be jest one of the jacks fer a day or two. You git me?'

Alf got him, and set off with the men, under the command of Aristide Papineau.

The camp was now almost completed, and the gang were engaged in driving the three-foot travoy roads through the bush, radiating toward the rollways at the brink of the gorge. The first snows had not yet fallen, though they were expected every day, and till then nothing could be done in the way of hauling. While the swampers grubbed out the tangles of dead ferns and blueberry, the sawyers accompanied them, keeping pace with them, and clearing the projected path of timber with saw and axe.

The whining of the cross-saws would cease suddenly. There would come shouts from the axemen: '*Garde l'arbre!*' Then the swampers would leap out of the way, and the tree would totter and come crashing down.

Aristide appeared to have forgotten the Papineau grudge against Alf. He greeted

127

him civilly, and put him to swamping. A number of the men were strung out along the route of a proposed travoy road, which was indicated by a line of blazed saplings. Alf was in front of them, and the task of each man was to advance and strike out the road along the course indicated.

Alf set to work and struggled with a stubborn tangle of matted sheep-laurel. Toward the middle of the morning, Pascal came up to him through the undergrowth. Alf was surprised to see that the man with him was Chamberland, wearing a bloody bandage round his head and carrying a grubbing tool in his hand.

'Eh, well, Monsieur Collet, so here we are, you see,' said Pascal, halting in front of him. 'Here is Chamberland, come to this, as I have had to come to it, and you, too, who are now no better than any of us. Listen, now, monsieur,' he continued, lowering his voice and gazing apprehensively about him. 'The men have been talking, and they have spoken about you. We know that it was not you who burned

Chamberland's house. We know that Smith made you one of the party in order that the men might hate you. But we know that you are with us. Well, monsieur, the men have become desperate and say that this cannot go on. And they wish to know whether you are on our side.'

He gave a side glance at Chamberland, who nodded assent.

'You see, monsieur, we are *Canayens*, we folk, and not dogs. And the men are desperate. But they are ignorant and Chamberland and Robitaille and — I, we are desperate men too. We need someone to lead us and tell us what we should do. If you would lead us, monsieur, it might help us very much. Monsieur — '

He came close up to Alf and whispered in his ear. Alf looked from the one man to the other in horror. The murderous scheme that Pascal had proposed was, indeed, that of a man driven to despair.

'No one will know, monsieur. It can be done so easily in the woods, and then Auguste Sorel would be on our side and permit us to have our farms again. So easily in the woods, monsieur, and everybody would think it was an accident — '

But Alf's mind recoiled from Pascal's plot to murder Egan. He couldn't stoop to that. He turned on Pascal angrily.

'I'm no murderer, Pascal!' he exclaimed. 'I'm here to work for the company. So you two take yourselves off. And listen to me. I say nothing to anyone of what you have proposed to me, but if Mr. Smith dies by an accident, I inform the police. And don't come to me with such propositions again.'

Pascal and Chamberland looked at each other; they drew off, exchanging words in a low tone that did not reach Alf's ears. They went back side by side along the travoy road, whispering to each other. Once, before disappearing in the undergrowth, they turned and looked back.

Alf turned to his work again. He was trying to see his way. But the events of the night before, and the discovery that the dead man had been Destry had thrown everything out of perspective. He did not know what to do, and it was impossible to go to Sorel.

The knowledge that Sorel had probably swindled Destry was not of the smallest use to Alf. And neither Sorel nor Egan was likely, under any circumstances, to confess his share in the murder.

The termination of the uncompleted travoy road was the crest of the hill, beneath which lay the home of Camille and Philippe, and the little settlement of burned out squatters. Alf, at the head of the line, drove hard toward it all through the afternoon. He was well in advance of the man behind him. Through the brush he occasionally heard one of the men calling to a companion, but he saw none of them again that day.

He worked furiously in order to banish his disturbing thoughts. It was nearing sunset when he drove the last yard of the travoy to the top of the crest, which was the boundary of the district that had been mapped out for cutting over that winter. In the thick of the forest it was nearly dark, but from the crest Alf could see the sunlight gilding the valley below.

Alf leaned upon his grubbing tool and gave way to the same sort of reverie as on that day when he escaped from the pen. So much had happened since then, and yet he was no further forward. He was still a wanted man. And he was playing a dangerous game to win his freedom. And arrest meant fingerprinting, and fingerprinting his detection and return to the pen. He had an immense desire to shake it all from him — disappear. His hopes, which had risen so high, had faded. It was as if he had walked into a blind alley. Why shouldn't he just drop his tool, leave the camp, and wander away?

He stood there, looking down, until the last glow of sunlight faded out of the valley below. Then he realised that the rest of the men must already be upon their homeward way. Well, he would keep up the fight. In a little while things would grow clear. Sorel must have discovered by now that his safe had been forced. Something was bound to eventuate, and he would know better then what course to follow. He shook himself together, and turned to retrace his steps along the travoy path.

As he turned, he heard a crackling in the underbrush. Two men stepped out of it and confronted him. One of them was Aristide, the other Alphonse Papineau. In their hands were their steel-heeled clubs. Aristide also carried a saw, but on sighting Alf he laid this deliberately down on the ground. The flexible riband curled like a bright snake among the dead ferns. The two men stood there looking at him, their mouths widening into grins.

'Well, Collet, I guess we got you now,' said Alphonse in simple statement.

Alf looked from the one face to the other, and he saw the plain intent of murder stamped upon each. And in that moment some knowledge came to him that heartened him, both to win this coming fight, and to go through hell to get Egan. For he knew by a sure instinct that this was no plan suddenly concocted between the two men, but of Egan's ordering.

Egan had planned it, Egan had sent the Papineaus there to murder him, because he had served Egan, incriminated Egan, and was no longer of any use to him. It was Egan's way to discard those who had served his purposes. It was the case of the penitentiary over again.

With that a mist flickered before Alf's eyes, and, without a word, suddenly assuming the offensive, Alf leaped at Alphonse, who was the nearer of the two men.

Taken by surprise, Alphonse tried to swing back his club, but the movement came too late. Alf's fist crashed into the man's face with fearful force, administering a clean knockout. Alphonse dropped to the ground as if he had been pole-axed. Alf ducked and leaped aside instinctively as he regained his footing, and at that moment Aristide's club went flashing downward. Had he been in the way that blow would have brained him. As it was, the club struck the ground with a force that sent it flying out of Aristide's hand.

The next moment Alf had leaped at Aristide in turn. He drove a succession of hammering right and left blows into Aristide's face. But he might as well have been attacking a cigar-store Indian for all the impression that his blows created. They resounded from Aristide's face as if from wood. They appeared to be absolutely ineffectual. Aristide did, indeed, give ground slowly before them, but he received them without wincing, all the while yelling to his son, the while his long, gorilla-like arms threshed like flails as he sought to clasp Alf in their embrace.

It was like a man fighting a bear, a bear that did not fight back, but watched its chance to gather its enemy into its clasp — the trap of the arms closed on its victim. Alf had grown incautious, had run in to administer the knockout. Now he was caught and dragged forward and hugged against Aristide's breast.

The old man's arms were steel and rubber. Alf could do nothing against that prodigious strength of clutch. And little by little it increased, and, ignoring Alf's battering blows, which covered his parrot beak and lips and hairy face with blood, Aristide began to squeeze the life out of his enemy. And all the while he shouted to Alphonse, and the bellows came from his bloody mouth as from some dreadful machine.

They wrestled to and fro. Alf's ribs, compressed into his lungs, hardly permitted him to breathe. Through the fog that obscured his vision Alf saw a look of triumph coming into the eyes in their sunken sockets. He saw the wolfish yellow fangs revealed in a bestial smile. He heard his thin breath whistling like wind. And beyond Aristide, over his shoulder, Alf saw Alphonse slowly rising from the ground in a half-dazed condition.

He heard Aristide still shouting to him, he saw the expression of understanding filter back into Alphonse's eyes, but all his senses were being crushed out of him by that bitter embrace, and he saw it all as in a picture, without any clear interpretation, except the sense of imminent danger.

He tried to pull himself together. He put forth all his failing strength into one final effort. With a quick upward thrust of his knee into Aristide's stomach, he succeeded in momentarily relaxing his enemy's hold. And, rushing in regardless of the closing arms, he hammered the bestial countenance above him till it disappeared in blood. He set his thews and back in the supreme struggle. He freed himself completely, drew in a chestful of air, and, with a last blow, sent Aristide reeling backward. And slowly, to Alf's intense surprise, the monster of a man tottered, swayed like a falling tree, and then went crashing to the ground, and lay there.

The next moment Alphonse's club descended upon Alf's head from behind, and the light of the world went out in a bright whirl of circling stars that faded into blackness.

Alf toppled, slipped, and went sliding down from the crest of the ascent into the valley below.

12

Opening the door of the log-house, late at night, to the familiar knocking, Camille Destry stood watching the figure of the man who lolled and reeled outside, a little hardness in her eyes, no pity in the little lines about her mouth.

It was a man in his late twenties, fair-haired, with a body well-proportioned and cast in a strong mould. The face showed breeding, but it was weak and vacuous, dissipated and furtive, and the consciousness of wasted years seemed to be stamped both in the hangdog look and in the irresolute, shuffling movements. As the man drew to the entrance, he raised his head and looked at his sister with a sort of abashed defiance.

'So you have been to Dupont's again, Philippe? Tell me, how many years have you come staggering home this way, like an animal?'

'Eh, well, how many years? As many as

138

I like!' he shouted with sudden anger. 'What else is there to do here since Auguste Sorel stole our lands?'

'Long before that — long before, Philippe,' his sister answered. 'And there is always work for a man in the world outside.'

'You wish me to go and leave you here unprotected?'

She might have made an ironical retort to this, but she only looked at him thoughtfully.

'I have been thinking of late it would be better for you to go, Philippe,' she said. 'Yes, I know I asked you to remain. But, as you say, there is nothing that you can do. You will find your supper on the kitchen table; eat it and go to bed, and perhaps we will discuss the matter in the morning.'

There was no doubting which was the stronger will.

Philippe Destry entered the house, but at the kitchen door he turned and faced his sister again. 'I am not going to take your orders any longer. Who are you to give orders to me? I am the seigneur, still the seigneur, do you understand that, Camille? Even though Sorel has stolen our father's lands.'

'Then why do you not force him to return them, or to account for them?'

'Name of dogs, what can I do? Have we the money to hire lawyers to fight him and the man Smith through all the courts of the land? You know it is the shame of it that drove me to what I am doing, after I had reformed.'

'Well, it doesn't matter, Philippe,' replied his sister after a little pause. 'There is perhaps nothing to be done, as you say. I am sorry I spoke harshly to you. Go to bed now.'

'You despise me, but when our father was alive — ' Philippe began; but she turned on him with a swift gesture.

'Philippe, I never wish to hear our father's name on your lips. It is my one request of you. You know that.'

The look she shot at him was unconsciously one of singular intensity; it seemed to search him to the soul. There seemed an unspoken question burning in her eyes, which for a moment he tried, half-defiantly, to meet. But then, dropping his head and hunching his shoulders, the drunkard shuffled inside the cabin.

Camille remained standing at the door in the darkness. From the lighted shacks about her came the sounds of voices faintly, of women washing up after the evening meal, crackling of sticks, chinking of cups, scolding of children. The ring of forest about the lonely valley seemed to lean ominously inward toward the little settlement, as if threatening it. Camille's face grew increasingly bitter as she stood there.

It had been more than four years since her father had gone to America — gone to his death at the hands of some murderous ruffian, with all the ensuing calamities that had come to her brother and herself. Before that, life had been altogether different. There had been the seigniorial life on the estate, the car, the frequent trips to Montreal, the opera, friends — all that had been wiped out, all their friends had forgotten them in their misfortunes as the sinister figures of Sorel and Smith rose on their horizon.

There had been Smith's designs upon herself, which Camille understood very well, and the burnings of the cottages in spite, because of her refusal to become his wife. In that remote corner of the province, there existed no public opinion to which it was possible to appeal. Smith and Sorel were slowly squeezing her to death, and her father's people.

Even yet she had not entirely come to realise the hopelessness of it. There was always the feeling that it would come to an end some time that the old days would return. But the time was at hand when evil would be met with violence. Camille knew very well what plans were being mooted among the *habitants*. Patient and long-suffering, once they were aroused they would wreak as savage a revenge as in the days of the rebellion.

And Philippe — but there she had established a blank wall across the current of her thoughts. She refused resolutely to let her mind dwell upon her brother. That evening was the first time in months that she had alluded to his drinking. She would never allude to it again. Since their father's death she had hidden her pride in silence toward him.

But in her desperation she had appealed to Sorel; then she had come upon the Yankee, Collet, Smith's newest recruit, burglarising the safe. She had supposed he was after money, and that it would not be difficult to persuade him to hand to her those papers that might shed light on the transactions between her father and Sorel. His refusal to let her have the papers had dumbfounded her; all that day she had alternated between despair and desperate schemes.

As she stood there at the door, voices hailed her, and out of the darkness she perceived two men approaching the house, carrying something between them. This disclosed itself as the body of a man, the body of Collet, and she recognised the bearers as Pascal and Chamberland.

They laid him down upon the wooden floor of the tiny porch. 'Eh, mademoiselle,' began Pascal, 'he is hurt, badly hurt. So we have brought him here, mademoiselle.'

Camille looked into Alf's unconscious face, at the bloodstained rags about his head. For the first moment, the thought of having him in her house was intolerable. Then she saw the advantage of it; but then the sense of necessity and hospitality swept this thought away.

'Carry him in,' she said. 'My room, Chamberland, at the rear.'

There were four small rooms besides the kitchen in the one-storey log building. Pascal and Chamberland carried in Alf's body and laid it on Camille's bed, removing the outer clothing, while Camille hurried into the kitchen and began boiling water to wash his wounds.

Philippe, having finished his supper, looked stupidly in, and then went to his room. When Camille removed the blood-soaked bandages, she uttered an exclamation of dismay. The iron-shod club had torn a great rent in Alf's scalp, and he had bled profusely. His pulse was small, his breathing hurried and shallow. She cleansed the wound with hot water, cutting away some of his hair, then fastened the edges with adhesive.

'It is a bad wound, but I do not think it is dangerous, mademoiselle,' said Chamberland. 'It is like mine.' He pointed to the soiled, bloodstained bandage about his own head. 'The skull is not broken. I examined it well.'

'How did he hurt himself?' asked Camille.

'It was the Papineaus, mademoiselle.'

'The Papineaus? But this is one of Smith's men.'

'No, mademoiselle. He is with us,' replied both men together.

'That is why Smith sent the Papineaus to kill him,' Pascal explained. 'Chamberland and I saw them slinking back into the woods as we were all going home, and as Monsieur Collet was not with us, we suspected that they had some evil plan in their minds. We followed them, mademoiselle. There was a fight between them and Monsieur Collet. It was Alphonse Papineau who struck him down from behind with his club. Monsieur Collet fell down the precipice. Aristide had brought a saw with him, and those devils sawed through a large tree, while we watched them, and directed its fall so that it should crush Monsieur Collet as he lay on the slope. But it did not fall on him. Then they would have descended and finished their work, but Chamberland and I appeared, and they did not dare to.'

'Yes, that is so, mademoiselle,' said Chamberland.

'But — did not Auguste Sorel and Smith send for him to come up here and help the Papineaus?' demanded Camille in bewilderment.

'We do not know. We do not understand it, mademoiselle,' answered Pascal. 'But we know that he is with us.'

Camille looked at Alf, lying motionless upon her bed, with less of horror and antipathy than she had felt for him before. 'But you — was he not one of the men who burned your home?' she asked Chamberland.

'He was *with* the Papineaus — yes, mademoiselle. But he had no hand in the burning and he is with us,' Chamberland replied with conviction.

'Mademoiselle,' Pascal interposed, 'you — you know what is being said among the men, that these conditions can go on no longer. And this will bring matters to a head. The Papineaus are afraid of us now, on account of what they did tonight, and will stop at nothing.'

'I know,' replied Camille. 'But what is there to be done?'

'Mademoiselle, there is not one of us who does not hate Auguste Sorel; but, after all, he is one of our people, turned bad. He is not like Smith. If it could be possible to approach him — '

'I have seen him,' answered Camille. 'He will do nothing. He takes his orders from Smith. No, nothing can be done.'

They looked at each other, then withdrew, muttering. When they had already left the house, Camille went to the door and called them.

'Listen!' she said vehemently. 'Tell the men that they must endure it a little longer. They must do nothing rash until — till I have had a chance to talk to Monsieur Collet. It may be that he is in a position to help us all. At any rate, I promise you I will do everything in my power — if they will wait a little longer.'

'*Ah, bien*, mademoiselle!' cried the two men exultantly.

And, since their faith in her was limitless, they departed cheerfully for their camp. Camille turned back and stood looking down at Alf. She was moved to deep compassion. He looked hardly more than a boy. He did not appear to be the ruffian she had imagined.

All night she sat beside him, watching and tending him; and all night she fought back consideration of her problem: did her pledge to Pascal and Chamberland involve yielding to Smith? That thought was one she could not face, because she knew she could not face that prospect.

13

A little before the dawn, Alf opened his eyes and came back to consciousness. He stared at Camille and about the little room, then tried to sit up in bed.

'You have met with an accident,' said Camille, bending over him. 'Pascal and Chamberland found you and brought you here last night. There is nothing to fear now, and I shall take care of you till you are better.'

Alf tried to speak, but dozed off again into a lighter coma. In this again he fought for his life with the Papineaus, he felt Aristide's strangle-clutch about his body; he sat up, choking, to feel Camille's cool hand upon his forehead. He heard her voice, telling him that all was well.

Through this delirium, his mind was working out the problem of the papers. He came back to full consciousness at last, to find the sun streaming in through the little window. Camille still sat beside him, but she had fallen asleep in her chair. In sleep, the bitterness that had engraved its lines upon her face had given place to earlier impressions. Alf, looking at her, saw something fine and wistful about her mouth and eyes, something that somehow reminded him of his mother and brought a sudden lump into his throat.

As he looked at her, Camille opened her eyes and saw that he was awake. Instantly the hard mask replaced that look that Alf had seen, but not quick enough to drive away the impression of it.

'Mademoiselle, about those papers — ' Alf began.

'Never mind now,' she answered.

'You did not understand me when we met on the road. I didn't go to Sorel's house to steal his money. I wanted those papers, too, but not for the same reason as yourself.'

'Well, never mind; you shall tell me when you get well.' But there was most evident eagerness upon her face. To Alf's mind, the situation seemed in some way to be clarifying. Whatever he could do

150

must, he felt, be done in alliance with Camille.

'I took all of them. It was Smith who sent me. He wanted evidence to show that Sorel had defrauded you of these lands.'

She looked at him intently.

'I wanted to find evidence of — something else. But I didn't find it. I gave Smith the worthless papers. I've hidden the rest.'

'Where?' Camille could not resist the query that broke from her lips.

'Under a board in my shack. I was thinking, if someone could get them and bring them here, you and I could go through them together and then talk things over.'

'Pascal will go — or Robitaille,' she cried eagerly.

'We'll have to be quick about it. If Smith discovers that he hasn't got the papers he thinks he has, he'll make some move. We've got to get our move in first.'

'I'll tell Pascal. He'll find them and bring them here. What is it you hope to find in them?' she continued.

151

'I — I can't answer that,' said Alf weakly. 'Do you think you can trust me just the same and let's work together?'

She scanned his face dubiously for a few moments. 'Yes, I think I can trust you, and I'll work with you,' she answered. 'After all, there's nobody else I can trust who is able to help me.'

Alf's strength came back rapidly. Two days later he was up and about, a little weak still from the loss of blood, but rapidly recovering. Those few days were the most peaceful Alf had ever known since his childhood. It was pleasant to sit in the little living-room with Camille, the sense of intimacy and home produced by a woman's presence. Philippe left the house early every afternoon, returning late at night in a half-drunken state. This threw them entirely on their own resources. They became almost intimate within the few days of Alf's convalescence. And one afternoon Camille began to speak of her brother and her father.

'If Philippe were different from what he is,' she said, 'something might have been done long ago. And he wasn't always like this. He was headstrong, but not weak, as he is now. He and his father never got along together. They quarreled dreadfully as he grew older. Philippe was wild. He ran away from school in Montreal, and he refused either to adopt a profession or to settle on the land and take up the care of the estate. Had he done so we might have dispensed with Auguste Sorel, and all this wretchedness would never have come upon us. But all Philippe wanted was money to spend in dissipation in Montreal.

'My father was weak and indulgent because he was so fond of him. He gave him money again and again, and Philippe would go to Montreal and squander it in gambling and drinking and evil living. Then he would come back humble and repentant and after a while my father would give him more. But it always went the same way. He had no strength of will where his affections were concerned, and he always hoped Philippe would reform.

'At last, however, he saw that he would have to be severe, for my brother's good. He gave him a large sum of money

— three thousand dollars — and told him not to come home again until he had a position. Within two months Philippe was back, and all his money was gone.

'He had counted on my father's eternal kindness, but this time he had counted wrong. My father refused to take him in. He gave him the fare back to Montreal, and a few dollars over. There was a terrible quarrel, and in the course of it he struck my father. He imagined that my father was a very rich man, with unlimited means, and it was just at the time of his worst embarrassment, just before he went south — to his death. Philippe did not believe his father's supply of money could ever come to an end.'

Her voice trembled as she went on. 'My father was brutally murdered. His money — if he had any — was stolen. Auguste Sorel declares the money paid my father was only a few hundred dollars — that all the rest went to discharge his liabilities. We shall never know the truth of that. They caught his murderer, and he is now serving a life sentence in a prison somewhere in America. He will never tell the truth, he could not be brought here and made to tell the truth.'

'No,' said Alf in a low voice.

'And for months and months we did not know my father was dead. Nobody identified him. Finally Monsieur Sorel got in touch with the authorities, and he was identified at the exhumation, by a ring he wore — my mother's. It was all terrible. And then we were driven from our home, and the man Smith came, and the burnings began — '

She burst into silent weeping. Alf turned away heartsick. Suppose she knew he was the man of whom she had spoken! Would she believe him, would she listen to him?

Alf had met with a grudging recognition from Philippe on the infrequent occasions of their meeting. He found it impossible to understand Camille's brother. The man did not appear to be a weakling; but the loss of the lands, and the sense of impotence which this loss had bred in him, seemed to have paralysed him mentally. He passed the mornings in a sort of irritable torpor, leaving the house after the midday meal for his libations. For the noisy, convivial drunkard there is hope; but drunkenness seemed to implant a sort of stealthy cunning in Philippe. Between him and his sister, there seemed to be a truce based upon passive contempt on the one side, and grudging acknowledgment on the other.

Certainly Camille was the man of the family. If she had much money remaining, she hoarded it religiously. Money was hardly needed in that simple life they led, except for the barest necessities. It was certain that none of the money with which Philippe purchased his liquor came from her. And the place where Philippe drank, Dupont's, was of ill repute.

The proprietor had set up his shebeen on a promontory three miles up the river, and it was frequented by lumbermen who often came twenty miles or more for the attractions Dupont had to offer them. However, none of the Sorel & Smith employees were in a position to supply their discredited seigneur with either whisky or the funds for securing it.

Alf had an inkling of the solution of this mystery on the afternoon of his conversation with Camille, but it left him with a strong sense of disquietude and uneasiness. Camille was attending at the home of a woman who had an ailing child, and Alf left the house for the first time, and made his way across the valley with a view to investigating it.

It was nothing more than the instinct which impels the woodsman to endeavour to discover the lie of the land, and the condition of the timber. The valley, Alf had learned, was Government land, and lay outside the boundaries of the Destry limits; hence the settlers there were safe from Sorel & Smith. Upon the farther ridges the forest began again, extending without a break through a territory that had never been logged over, perhaps five hundred miles northward.

Seated upon the ridge, Alf surveyed this district with all the woodsman's enthusiasm. It was not its commercial possibilities that attracted him, but the vivid sense of the unknown, of virgin land, the instinct of the pioneer. It made

157

him happy, it drove all cares away from his mind temporarily. It was while he was seated there that he perceived two men coming slowly along the valley underneath, in his direction.

One was Philippe, who had left the house a short time before, and was presumably on his way to Dupont's drinking den. The other, to his astonishment and chagrin, Alf recognised as Alphonse Papineau. They had evidently met by appointment. Standing there, hidden by a turn of the valley from the view of the settlers, they were only visible to Alf, above them.

They stood there, apparently engaged in argument. Not a word of their voices was audible to Alf at that height above them, but it was clear from their gestures that Philippe was demanding something, and Alphonse reluctantly, or with feigned reluctance acceding. At length Alphonse put his hand to his coat and passed something to Philippe. The gesture was as if money had passed.

Then, taking Philippe by the shoulders, Alphonse proceeded to speak to him with threatening and emphatic movements of his head. Finally he turned abruptly away and went off up the hillside in the direction of the company limits, while Philippe made his way along the valley in the direction of the riverine road that led to Dupont's.

It was clear Philippe was so far lost to self-respect that he had been willing to take money from Egan's man. And Egan was not supplying him with money for the gratification of his desire for nothing.

Alf made his way back to the log house in a state of profound dejection. Treachery was impending. And he dared not mention what he had seen to Camille.

14

On the next night Pascal appeared at the house, carrying the package, which he had found where Alf had deposited it. Alf proposed to open it immediately, but Camille, though she was as eager as he to take up the matter, dissuaded him.

'Let us wait till tomorrow,' she insisted. The next day they went through the papers. They covered a period of years. Alf pointed out to Camille the facts on which he based his inferences of fraud. There were receipts from Destry for large sums of money that Sorel had paid to him, but there was a discrepancy of thousands between these sums and the seigneur's income from houses in Montreal and bonds and shares, all of which appeared gradually to have been disposed of.

'You see, there is no deed to the property,' said Alf. 'There is no proof whatever that your father assigned it to him. And there are discrepancies which furnish *prima facie* evidence of fraudulent dealings on Sorel's part. One thing is evident to me from these papers: Sorel can be compelled to give you a complete accounting of all the business transactions that he had with your father.'

'Not now,' answered Camille.

'Why not?'

'He can plead that the papers have been stolen. Even if they are returned to him, he can claim, which will be the truth, that they have not been returned intact.'

'I guess I made a pretty bad mistake in dividing them,' said Alf. 'I was playing for my own hand — if I'd known about you, or thought about it from your point of view, of course . . . Well, we must convict Sorel from these papers if at all.'

'Mr. Collet, won't you tell me why you wanted these papers?' Camille asked. 'I — of course I don't want to try to probe into your affairs, but we must be frank with each other if we are to be of much use to each other.'

For a moment, Alf trembled on the

verge of a decision. He checked himself in time. He knew there was no possibility of inducing Camille to believe his story. On the contrary, he would only succeed in awakening all her suspicions.

'It's nothing connected with the property,' he answered. 'It's — it's a personal matter between myself and Smith. I came up here in the hope of finding him. I found him. These papers don't give me the clue I wanted. But I want to help you to get back your land.'

Camille looked at him again for a moment in that dubious way; she said no more upon the subject, but Alf knew that she was not satisfied.

'Well, what do you think we can do?' she asked.

'Go to Sorel. Have it out with him. Threaten legal proceedings on the strength of what evidence we have managed to secure.'

'Tell him we have his papers, then?'

'Yes. He must know anyway.'

Camille looked doubtful. 'Mr. Collet,' she said suddenly, speaking with intense conviction, 'there is more to all this than appears upon the surface. I am convinced of that. I believe that if Auguste Sorel has committed a fraud, he would be willing to compromise with me. You heard my conversation with him the other night. I offered to confirm his claim to the lands if he would only let the people go back to their farms. He rejected my offer. No, Smith has him, bound hand and foot, in some way that we don't understand. I — I don't know that I want to understand,' she added fearfully. 'I — am afraid — that it's something about my father's death.'

'If Sorel and Smith are bound together, can we break that bond by these papers?' asked Alf. 'That's the entire situation. I think we should confront Sorel with these papers and have a showdown. Tell him that unless he renders you an accounting you will secure legal representation. We don't have to settle his relations with Smith.'

'It will have to come to that. These conditions can't last, Mr. Collet. The men are planning something desperate — arson and murder. Whatever we are going to do must be done at once.'

'For that and for another reason,' said Alf. 'Smith thinks his time has come to play his own hand. We must forestall him.'

'His own hand?' Camille stared at him, and Alf saw that she had grown white to the lips.

'To oust Sorel. He appears to think that he is in a position to do so with the papers that he possesses. That is why he made me steal them for him. But we've checkmated him there, because the papers that he has are worthless to him. Yes, we must act at once. Today.'

'Tomorrow. You are not strong enough yet. Another day will make all the difference in the world to you.'

'Tomorrow, then.'

Camille hesitated. 'He hopes to get the property out of Sorel's hands?' she asked. 'Did he — did he say anything more about his — expectations?' She looked keenly into Alf's face. 'Yes, Mr. Collet, I see that he did. That man is the only person on earth whom I'm afraid of.

'I'm going to tell you something. About three years ago, soon after he came here.

He — he tried to make love to me. I repulsed him, and he told me then, and I could see he meant it, that he had never in his life been baffled in anything that he meant to have. He meant to have me, he said, however long he waited. After that he was always respectful whenever we met, and I thought he had forgotten, or made an empty threat. Then, a few months ago, he asked me again. He told me the time would soon be at hand. I didn't know what he meant. Then, after I had refused him again, these burnings began, and he let me understand that only I could stop them.

'I refused, and they went on. The whole countryside was terrorised. With any people less patient than ours there would have been an outbreak long ago.'

'He can do nothing more.'

'Oh, you don't know!' she cried. 'He has some trump card that he has not yet shown. He has intimated as much to me. I don't know what it is. And I won't know!' she cried defiantly. 'It is — something monstrous that he has hinted at. Something that will put me altogether within his power.'

'He's *bluffing*,' said Alf contemptuously. 'I know the man mighty well, mademoiselle, and I tell you he's bluffing. Tomorrow you and I'll go to Sorel. We'll tell him what we've agreed on. If he refuses — do you know what I've been thinking? I'll tell you. Possession is nine points of the law. Why shouldn't it be possible for us to take a leaf out of Sorel's book and seize the lands and the mill for you, and let them prove it's theirs? The men would follow us.'

'You — you think that's possible?' cried Camille, looking at him with parted lips.

'Our men could make pretty quick work of Smith and the Papineaus. And look at it this way: it might prevent an outbreak, and perhaps murder.'

Camille reflected. 'Anyway, we must see Sorel first,' she said, 'and then we shall know. If only it had been possible to get Philippe to do something. He isn't a coward — I don't want you to think that of him — but ever since these troubles have come upon us his will and initiative have seemed paralysed. And' — she

166

dropped her voice — 'I have almost been afraid that Smith has some hold over him. Where does he get the money for the *whisky blanc* he buys? Not from me! He must spend as much on it each week as would keep us all two or three months.'

They were standing at the door of the log cabin in the mellow morning. The valley lay before them, so peaceful in the clear sunshine, and everything was so still that they could hear the faint drilling of a woodpecker in a dead tree far up the hillside. Camille turned to Alf again.

'I wish with all my heart that I could always live in a peace like this,' she said. 'It is so senseless, all this struggling and conspiring, when Nature gives us all that anyone has need of.' She sighed. 'But tomorrow we shall know,' she said.

After dinner she went down to the colony to see the sick child of one of the *habitants* whose home had been burned down, a formerly fairly prosperous farmer named Tremblay. The child was under-nourished and puny, and the whole afternoon Camille spent with the mother, cleaning the wretched shack and looking

167

after the swarming brood, and advising her and promising aid. The service momentarily drove the thought of the morrow out of her mind. But when she started on her homeward way, at sundown, the memory came over her, producing a sick revulsion.

She hated it all, the righting of the wrong no less than the wrong. She would have abandoned the fight, everything, but for those outcasts in the valley who were her people, bound to her by ties of immemorial generations.

As she approached the cabin, she saw a man descending the gorge opposite, which formed the boundary of the Destry lands. He was coming into the valley, and as Camille watched him she saw that he was bound, apparently, for her home. And now she could distinguish the deformed shoulder, the barrel-like body, the long pendulous arms. She shuddered as she awaited him at the door. She had never overcome her horror of Egan; and now it almost looked as if he meant to take the initiative in the showdown.

She heard him whistling as he came toward her, and her blood seemed to congeal at the thought of being forced into marriage with him.

She would never consent; and yet, at the back of her decision there was a horror which had never shaped itself in her mind clearly, but remained always a dim, nebulous, phantom shape beneath the surface of her consciousness colouring it without controlling it.

Egan came up and greeted her with feigned heartiness. 'Afternoon, mademoiselle!' he called. 'I jest came to pay a little friendly visit, seein' it's so long since I was here before, and to thank you fer takin' in that man Collet of mine. How's he gettin' along?'

'Monsieur Collet is much better — he is nearly well again,' she answered in a constrained voice.

'That's good news,' said Egan. 'Kind of a nasty accident he had, bein' hit by that there tree which had been sawed three-quarters of the way through and then left standin'. It's a fort'nate thing those men of mine found him the way they did, or he might have laid there fer days.'

'No thanks to you, he didn't!' Camille cried vehemently. 'Mr. Smith, there's no reason why I shouldn't be frank with you. I know that you sent those two ruffianly Papineaus to murder him!'

Egan uttered an oath.

'And they would have completed their job — the job *you* gave them.' Camille went on, 'if those two other men hadn't arrived upon the scenes in time. Yes, you know that I'm speaking the truth. And for that reason itself this house holds no welcome for you!'

Egan scowled. 'So that's what that Collet's been feedin' you on since he's been here, is it, Mademoiselle!' he sneered. 'Kind of took up with him, have you? He sure must have made himself strong with you, mademoiselle, if you're willin' to believe that sort of lie a hobo pitches you.'

'They are not lies, and I don't know what you mean by a 'hobo.''

'A tramp. A bum. That feller's seen the inside of more'n one jail, mademoiselle,

170

from what he told me himself. 'Course, he may have been delirious when Pascal and Chamberland found him, and mebbe believed them notions he'd been dreamin' was the truth. But more likely than not he was jest lyin' because him and me had a few words that mornin' before he went to work, about some of the men's socks havin' disappeared — '

'Oh, you cheap liar!' cried Camille, flushing.

'All right,' said Egan. 'We'll let it go at that. But as fer plottin' to kill that precious Clarence of yours, the Papineaus was both with me on the other side of the limits the afternoon that Collet hurt himself, and we're all prepared to swear to it.'

'It isn't hard to swear to a lie,' Camille answered contemptuously. 'I don't know who'd believe the Papineaus.'

'Meanin' me, too, I suppose?' asked Egan menacingly.

'Meaning the lot of you,' Camille answered, facing him without flinching. 'A man's known by the company he keeps.'

Egan grinned savagely, and shot his hands out, seizing Camille by the wrists. 'See here now, mademoiselle,' he began, 'quarrelin' don't lead nowhere. You and me's goin' to talk to each other straight.'

'Let my wrists go!'

She stood there, quite passive, but she dominated him by sheer moral force. A hideous look came over Egan's face, but he released her.

'Remember soon after I first come here I asked you to marry me?' he demanded. 'Oh, you needn't wince,' he went on, seeing her involuntary shrinking, and flushing darkly. 'I'm jest as good as any other man, and a darn sight better than some. At any rate, I never been a hobo. Well, I told you then I'd git you sooner or later, and that I always got what I went after. Well, that time's come now. I want you.'

'I tell you that I'll *never* be your wife. Don't you see that I *hate* you?'

'Sure, an' that suits me down to the ground,' responded Egan, grinning more easily. 'And now, if the preliminary sparrin's over, I'll talk straight to you and

172

show you where your interest lays. Sorel's finished. He swindled your father right and left for years, and I got the papers to prove it.'

A feeling of thankfulness came over her. So Smith had not yet learned that in this respect he had been checkmated.

'And Sorel's goin' to hand back those lands — to me,' Egan continued. 'And if you want to git back your position fer yourself and your brother, you're goin' to git it back through me, by marryin' me. Sorel's goin' and you and me's goin' to be bosses of this territory. There'll be a car fer you, and pretty dresses, and dia-monds, mebbe — anything you want, if you'll be sensible. You got to marry someone, ain't you? Which of these folks d'you reckon is goin' to hitch up with you? Collet?'

'Oh, you are a brute!' cried Camille.

'Well, what's the matter with me?' continued Egan, apparently surprised that this recitation had produced no effect.

'It's simply that I don't care for you — more than that, I hate you!'

'Shucks!' retorted Egan. 'You leave the

love part of the business to me, I guess I kin attend to that!'

Suddenly, as if driven by overpowering passion, he advanced and seized her in his arms. 'Camille, honey I've got you at last!' he cried. 'I've got to have you! God, I'd go through hell fer you! I've gone through hell fer you!'

She struggled and cried out. Above her she saw Egan's face, distorted with passion. A hideous terror of the man weakened her and made her helpless.

15

When Philippe left the house that afternoon, a little later than usual, Alf waited until he had crossed the valley and then followed him. It was his intention to go to Dupont's in the hope, slight though it was, of picking up anything that might be learned, particularly as to Philippe's relations with the Papineaus.

He sighted Philippe at the point where the trail dipped toward the river gorge, and then followed leisurely, keeping him occasionally in view, until he arrived outside Dupont's shack at sunset.

It was the cheapest and flimsiest construction, a temporary structure erected at that convenient point for dispensing liquors smuggled across Lake St. Laurent. The only thing of any value that Dupont possessed, apart from his stock, which was worth, apart from Prohibition prices, just about as much as hat varnish was a fast motorboat

175

capable of holding half-dozen passengers. Dupont kept it moored at the landing below the shebeen, ready to flee upstream in case of any unexpected raid on the part of revenue officers.

It was Saturday evening, and even as Alf watched from among the trees in which he had taken up his position, the lumberjacks began trooping up from the company huts. Half a dozen of them entered the place within a quarter of an hour, and their numbers were swelled by the occupants of a large row-boat, filled to the gunwales, containing a party from some distant camp, with one or two trappers whom they had picked up on their way.

The inside of the place poured out a stream of light through the two windows from the large oil lamps. Shouting arose. The lumberjacks were getting drunk as quickly as they could in preparation for the evening. There was no wheel, for all the money that circulated found its way into Dupont's liquor-till, but two or three petty games for small stakes — poker and dice, and blackjack — were starting in the farther end of the place, under the supervision of Dupont's two loutish sons. Two or three women who had spent the summer there, ostensibly as boarders, began to circulate among the crowd of roisterers. Alf could see Dupont himself, a little foxy man with a red beard, presiding over the bar, his shifty eyes roaming from one group to another as he calculated his profits.

Alf was considering whether or not to enter when suddenly the door opened, and a woman came out as if propelled by a violent shove. She staggered, caught one of the posts that supported the roof of the little stoop, and clung to it for a moment, looking back with an amazed, stupid expression at the man who followed her.

The next instant, Alf saw that it was Egan. He had not seen him enter the place; he must have been there before the lumberjacks began to arrive; the inference Alf might have drawn, which would have been correct, was that Egan was the proprietor and Dupont his dummy.

Egan followed the woman and marched up to her, his chin thrust forward in the ward-bully's way. Alf, from where he stood, could plainly hear every word that was spoken.

'Now I've had about enough of this!' Egan said in English. 'I'm tired of it, and tired of bein' pestered by you!'

The woman answered in English with a strong French accent: 'I love you, Jeem! I love you!' And she repeated it again and again, as if that sentence explained and atoned for everything.

'I told you what I'd do fer you. I'll pay your passage back to Montreal. Whatcha mean by comin' back here after I told you I was tired of seein' you around?'

'Jeem, I love you!'

'I tell you I'm sick of that swan-song of yours. I acted fair with you and sent you home to Montreal.'

'That isn't my home. My home is on the other side of Lake St. Laurent. You *know* it was because of you my father closed his doors on me. And I was to have been married to my Charles in one month's time, before you got hold of him in the city. He'd been working there and saving up the money for our home, and what did you do to him? Why hasn't he *dared* come back since then? And you *promised* me that you'd make me your wife, when you came to me with false messages from Charles, and false promises, and made me love you.'

'Yep, that's an old song,' said Egan. 'Change it, or put on a new needle, Celeste. Honest, I'm sick of it, and of your face. Now see here! I'll send you back to Montreal. You can get a job there. You don't have to come botherin' me, because what I told you I meant — '

'Jeem, don't you love me at all? Can't you love me? Don't you remember?'

Egan seized her by the shoulders and gave her a vicious shaking. 'No!' he roared. 'Git *that* through your head, Celeste. And I won't have you around here — get that too. And — '

But suddenly, with an unearthly cry, she had shaken free of him, turned and ran down toward the gorge. Egan took a handkerchief from his pocket and wiped his forehead. 'My God, the little she-devil!' he muttered. He glanced after her irresolutely for a moment, and then, with a vicious scowl, turned abruptly from the shack and strode off along the trail. In a moment he was lost to view among the trees.

Alf waited an instant longer and then turned and made his way after Celeste. Perhaps twenty seconds had elapsed since her flight and Egan's disappearance. He could hear the dead twigs and ferns crackling under her feet as she hurried toward the gorge. As he hastened in pursuit of her, he saw her disappearing figure among the pines. He realised that she was in a condition of frenzy, and quickened his pace, but Celeste, looking back over her shoulder and evidently taking him for Egan, plunged frantically through the underbrush.

She was making for the rollways, and Alf, fearing that she was planning some desperate act, now pursued her at the top of his speed. He caught her upon the very brink of the gorge. She struggled furiously in his grasp.

'Let me go! Let me kill myself! I don't want to live, and you have no right to stop me!' she cried in French.

Alf only held her more closely. Suddenly she seemed to realise that he was not Egan. Her struggles ceased. She looked up at him with streaming eyes. 'Who are you? What do you want?' she cried.

'I want to save you from committing a foolish act.'

'Why shouldn't I? I've nothing to live for now. He cares for me no longer. He broke my life and drove me from my home.'

'Who? Smith?'

'Yes, Monsieur Smith! Listen, monsieur, and tell me if I am not right in wishing to die. Four years ago I was happy, I had a good home across the lake, and I was to have married Charles. He had gone to the big city across the boundary, and was making much money, to furnish our home. I was expecting him every day. Instead of him there comes Monsieur Smith with messages from Charles, that he has got into some trouble and dares not return, and I am to be good and wait for him. Then Monsieur Smith tells me it is no trouble, but here is another woman whom Charles loves. And I believe him. He tells me that he loves me. He wins my love. Then, when I beg him to marry me, he puts me off with excuses. My father turns me out of his home. He says he will kill Monsieur Smith if he shows his face in the village again. And so I — I am at Jeem's mercy.

'He sent me to Montreal, and kept me there, and used to come to see me, and all the time he told me some day he would marry me. But last month I became desperate. He had only given me a very little money, and I worked — I worked as a servant. At last I came back. I had told Jeem that I was coming, and when he could not prevent me he arranged for me to board with Monsieur Dupont. And then he — he lied about me to Dupont and the lumberjacks, and they thought I was other than what I am, and those other women there — *Ah Sainte Vierge*, have pity on me! What could I do?

'Now he tells me he loves me no more, and I am to go out of his life forever, and there is Charles, whom I have always loved, of whom I know nothing. And my father's home closed to me. Well, why should I not kill myself?'

'That's all foolishness,' said Alf, taking her by the arm and leading her, unresisting, from the rollways. 'We'll find your Charles for you somehow, and then everything will come out all right.'

'All right? How can it be all right? What would he have to say to me if he knew? No, no, it is finished, it is all finished!'

For a moment she seemed about to renew her desperate struggle, but again she ceased and began sobbing wildly, helplessly. Alf held her until the outburst had ceased.

'It's no use talking of killing yourself,' he said. 'The time will come when you'll be mighty glad you didn't. Now the first thing you've got to see is that Smith's finished with you. You've got to face it, it's no use deceiving yourself into thinking that someday he's going to suddenly start caring for you again. That isn't the way with men — or women either, I guess. When it's finished, it's finished. I guess you see that, don't you?'

'Oh, I know, I know! He does not care.

I have always known it. I was just his plaything. He is bad, bad. I wish to God that I had never seen his face!'

'Then,' said Alf, 'you must just go back to Dupont's — '

'I cannot go there. They make mock of me, all those men. They ask me when he is going to marry me. I cannot bear it any longer. Tonight, when he laughed at me, I knew it was the end!'

'You must go there for tonight,' said Alf. 'In the morning I will see what can be done for you. Just trust me, and I'll see you through some way — I'll see you through. Will you believe that?'

'Yes, I believe you,' she said, snatching at his hand and pressing it to her lips gratefully. 'And if ever I can do anything for you, like what you have done for me, I'll do it. No man has treated me the way you have done for long — never since they found out about Jeem and me.'

Alf accompanied her in silence back toward Dupont's place. Suddenly a thought came to him. 'There's one thing you can do for me now,' he said. 'What is your name?'

184

'Celeste Trudeau.'

'And this Charles of yours — his other name?'

'Bartel. Charles Bartel. Why do you ask? You know him?'

'No, I don't know him,' answered Alf. 'But I was wondering; are you sure it was another woman kept him from you, or do you think it may have been true, the message he sent you about getting into trouble?'

'I don't know, monsieur. It is all lies, lies everywhere where Jeem is concerned.'

'What trouble could he have got into down where he was, and why should that make him afraid to come back here? It must be Smith that he's afraid of.'

'I don't know. But I wish he would come. He would not marry me now, but perhaps he would pity me, say a kind word to me.'

They were approaching the shack again. From within the sounds of drunken laughter came to their ears. A fine snow had begun to fall; already the ground was white with it.

'Where do you sleep?'

'Here, monsieur,' said Celeste, pointing to a low annexe which Alf had not noticed before, at the back of the building. There were three low doors, leading into small cubicles, divided one from another by thin pine planks.

'You are safe there?'

'Safe? Yes, I am safe, but only because they know that I belong to Jeem. They would not respect me for myself — it is that they are afraid of him.'

'Go to bed, then. Tomorrow I shall see if something cannot be done for you. You promise me you will not try to do yourself any harm again?'

She promised him, and then, stifling a new outburst of weeping, fled into the little room and closed the door.

Alf felt a strange exaltation of spirits. Somehow he imagined that through Celeste he might find the clue which had thus far eluded him. But of course that was nonsense. He had simply burdened himself with an unnecessary task when he needed to put all his energy into the undertaking that Camille and he had set for themselves. He turned away, dismissing the thought of Celeste from his mind, with a shrug of pity and self-contempt for his weakness.

As he turned he saw Dupont, the proprietor, standing behind him, staring at him. As their eyes met, Dupont wagged his red beard and chuckled.

16

'Eh, a wet night, Monsieur Collet,' remarked Dupont, who evidently knew Alf by sight. 'The snow begins, and now the lumbering will start also.'

Alf brushed past the man and entered the shack. It was now packed with men. Nearly all of them were drunk, and pairs were dancing on the rough wood floor, embracing one another grotesquely, to the shrill tune that someone was striking out on a fiddle.

Alf looked about him and almost immediately saw Philippe, sitting between the two Papineaus in a corner. There was liquor in glasses before the three men. Philippe's head lolled forward on his shoulders, his eyes were closing; momentarily he would look up with a start as Alphonse whispered in his ear, and nod.

Alphonse and Aristide saw Alf almost as quickly as he saw them. As he approached them Alphonse squinted; his hand went to his belt.

Alf had no fear of an encounter. In the closely packed room, he believed he was a match for either man. But he was resolved to avoid one unless it was forced upon him. He went up to Philippe and clapped him on the shoulder. 'Come, Monsieur Destry,' he said. 'Your sister will be anxious about you.'

The two Papineaus burst into roars of laughter. The music stopped. Every face in the room was looking at them. Alf realised that, just as on that other occasion in the woods, this was a test; he was already matched against the Papineaus.

He must get Philippe away or lose face so that the men would not follow him in the event of Camille and himself deciding to seize the mill. And he had walked into this position without any plans; he had no excuse for taking Philippe away; he had gone to Dupont's without any formulated plans.

'Come, Monsieur Destry,' Alf repeated. 'This is no place for our seigneur to be drinking in.'

An electric shock seemed to run through Philippe. Alf had touched him in the one accessible spot, the remnants of his pride. 'That is so, Collet!' he cried, leaping up with a bound that overset the three tumblers and called forth curses from the Papineaus.

'Eh, Philippe, so you have become the Yankee's dog when he whistles, you follow him?' demanded old Aristide, scowling at Alf.

Philippe stopped and stared irresolutely at Alf; he was in that condition of intoxication when a man seizes on a mood and converts it into a determination.

'Eh, you stay here, Philippe!' shouted old Aristide, rising and clapping a huge paw on Philippe's shoulder.

'Come, Monsieur Destry,' said Alf for the third time. 'You do not wish to drink with your own *villeins* any longer.'

The word, carrying with it the memories of the *habitant's* condition of feudal peonage at a period not beyond the memories of the oldest men, stung like a sword-thrust. The group about the table started and growled. But Alf knew that he had won. Drawing Philippe's arm through his, he led him from the shebeen, without looking round, though he expected every instant to feel Alphonse's knife between his ribs. In the doorway stood Dupont, a grin carved on his bearded face; they were past him and tramping on the trail in the falling snow.

Some distance from the shack, Philippe stopped and stared at Alf. 'Who are you? What do you want here?' he mumbled.

'Monsieur Destry, I wished to see you when we could be alone, to ask you if you will not join your sister in her fight for the lands?'

'Fight?' hiccoughed Philippe in a shrill voice. 'What's the good of fighting? They've got us down. Let us live and let live, I say. Listen, I'll tell you something!' He grasped Alf by the arm. 'Sorel's reached the end of his rope. He doesn't know it yet, but he's going, he's going out like a dog, and Smith's going to be the company, and then there's good times coming for all of us. He's promised me — ' He broke off and looked at Alf with sudden suspicion. 'What are you asking me questions for?' he cried. 'What have you come here for? Whose spy are you?' There was an unmistakable note of fear in his voice. 'What do you want? By God, I'll make you answer me!'

'I want nothing from you,' answered Alf. 'I want to save your sister from becoming Smith's wife.'

Philippe leaped back as if he were stung. 'His wife?' he yelled. 'Camille? No, no, you are lying to me. Celeste — that woman Celeste is his woman. What does he want with — ? No, no, it is a lie. Damn you, I am the seigneur, and Camille is my sister!'

'All the more reason to protect her, then. Monsieur Destry, will you not strike a blow to protect her, and to help her regain the lands Sorel has stolen?'

'But Sorel is going, I tell you!'

'Against Smith, then?'

'Smith? No, no, it cannot be done! That man is a devil! Ah, you are trying to cross-question me! But I am not in the witness-box. No, no, it is a lie you tell me, about Smith and Camille!'

'Ask her.'

'It is a lie, I tell you,' repeated Philippe. 'My God, the man is a devil, but he is not such a devil as that!'

'It rests with you to do what you can to stop it.'

Philippe stood swaying drunkenly upon his feet. 'It — it cannot be done,' he whispered. 'We must run away, then. We must go by night. I shall speak to her — '

'There is no reason to run away. Monsieur Destry, you are not bound to the man Smith. Don't you see how he is playing upon your weakness, trying to use you for his purposes?' He laid a hand on his shoulder. 'Won't you remember that you should be the seigneur of these lands?' Alf pleaded. 'Won't you join us in what we are trying to do?'

'Get rid of Sorel? Yes, yes!'

'And Smith!'

The expression on Philippe's face was pitiful. 'He is a devil. It cannot be done,' he kept muttering. 'We must run away. I shall speak to her.'

Alf could get no more out of him. Torn between two purposes, Philippe was as weak as water; and in some way Egan seemed to have brought him completely under his influence.

They went on in silence after that. The fumes of the liquor were clearing from Philippe's brain, he walked more steadily, but he kept muttering in an undertone, he seemed panic-stricken by what Alf had told him.

They were nearing the house when suddenly they heard a cry come from the entrance. It was Camille's voice. Instantly Alf was running toward the place at full speed. He saw two shadows wrestling in the entrance. Camille was struggling in Egan's embrace. Alf launched himself at the man. But Egan was too quick for him. Alertly he released Camille, and assumed the prize fighter's position, crouching, ready to parry Alf's blow with his left arm. Crouching, squatting there in the darkness, he looked like some hideous monster, rather than a man.

As Alf was about to hurl himself upon him, Camille came swiftly between them. 'It's nothing, it's nothing, Monsieur Collet!' she cried. 'He — he startled me,

194

that is all. He meant no harm.'

She clung to Alf's arm and held him back, while Egan gradually resumed an upright posture again. 'So this is the new champeen, hey?' he jeered. 'Guess I did fergit myself when I tried to kiss you, mademoiselle, but I ain't the only man in the world's done *that*.'

Alf stood watching him grimly. How far Egan had tried to go he could not know, he had to accept Camille's word; above all, for her sake he was anxious not to precipitate the showdown with Egan — not now, not here.

'So *you're* mademoiselle's champeen, Collet!' Egan jeered, now in possession of himself again. 'Well, lemme tell you this. Jest as soon as you git back to camp I'm going to give you what's been owin' you fer a good while. I'm goin' to whale hell out of you in front of the whole gang, and the women too. I'm going to make you so low you'll be whinin' and cringin' and lickin' my shoes to let you go, before I've done with you. And then I'm goin' to kick you out of camp so hard you won't stop

195

travelling till you git over the border. And if you try to slink away by night, I'll git you if I follow you to the ends of the earth.'

'You won't have to follow me to the ends of the earth,' answered Alf. 'I'll be there tomorrow when you want me. I guess your attempt to carry out those dreams will be about as successful as your attempt to murder me.'

'You're lyin', you thievin' bum, you jailbird!' Egan shouted. 'Come on, I'll settle with you now!'

All at once Alf felt a vast coolness fill him. He knew that he was Egan's master. He had always known that. But now this cool understanding beat down the last sparks of rage in him and gave him caution and judgment. Not here! It must be before the men, that showdown; Alf would choose his own battlefield.

Again Camille was clinging to him; and then unexpectedly there sounded Philippe's voice out of the darkness. There was a new note of resolution in it.

'This won't do, Mr. Smith,' said Philippe. 'I can't have my sister insulted, nor any guest of ours either. Gentlemen, I must ask you to settle your quarrel somewhere else.'

'Say, where d'you git your hooch, Philippe?' asked Egan derisively. 'Must have been mighty strong, that last bottle, to make you talk like that. Say, you git back to it, and don't trouble what brains you got left about other folks' affairs,' he continued derisively. 'Jest listen here, Philippe!'

He shot a prehensile arm out of the darkness and drew Philippe toward him. He whispered something, and then his cackling laughter came out of the dark like a fiend's.

He turned to Camille. 'I'm sure sorry if I fergot meself, mademoiselle,' he said in mock apology. 'As fer you Collet, you scum, I'll settle with you tomorrow. And I guess that flea I put in your ear's goin' to stick, Philippe!'

He strode away into the valley, and for a few moments the three remained silent and motionless at the door of the house. Alf was fuming that he had not settled with Egan then and there, despite his realisation that his decision had been a wise one.

Camille read what was passing in his mind, and put her fingers on his arm. 'Monsieur Collet, you are too sensible to be willing to fight with a man like that,' she said. 'What he says is of no significance at all. Tomorrow we shall see Auguste Sorel. That is all that will matter.'

Philippe had left them. Alf stood with Camille in the dark little passageway. Some new and mighty force seemed to be shaking him, drawing him toward her.

'I let him go because you asked me to,' he said in a low tone, 'because I — I'd do anything on earth you asked me to.'

Their hands met and clasped. 'I know,' Alf heard her whisper.

Philippe's voice came to them out of the dark living room. 'For God's sake come in!' he cried. 'Let's get into the light! Light the lamp, Camille!'

They went inside. When Camille set the lighted lamp upon the table Alf read the conflict in Philippe's heart by the ghastly whiteness of his face.

17

Like a trapped wolverine, Sorel faced them in the little office of the mill the following afternoon, his china-blue eyes shifting from Alf's face to Camille's and back again.

'You do not need to tell me that you broke open my safe and stole my papers, Collet,' he said. 'You are a criminal, but you are worse than that, for you are a fool. You have played into the hands of Smith. When I employed you, you assured me that you were a loyal man. What did he pay you? You fool, if you had been faithful to me I would have given you far more money than you got from Smith! As for those papers that you stole, you can prove nothing by them — nothing at all. Bah, is it any wonder that your father was unable to hold his lands, Mademoiselle Destry? He was just such another fool.'

'Those papers,' said Alf, 'show clear evidence of fraud. It is for you to explain away the discrepancies if you can. And there is no deed to the property bearing Monsieur Destry's signature.'

'It's *registered* in Fall City!' snarled Sorel.

'Perhaps. But there is no deed. You cannot produce a deed. On the evidence of these papers we can obtain legal aid without preliminary expense, the obstacle you have been counting on.'

''We?'' sneered Sorel. '*Hein?* 'We'?' There was a look of intense malice in the china-blue eyes as he glanced again from Alf to Camille. 'So it appears that you are in love with this Yankee adventurer, mademoiselle, this burglar who has fled here from his own country to escape imprisonment for crime? And soon the marriage bells will ring, *hein*, Mademoiselle Destry? My congratulations — yes, my warm congratulations! Your father would have been pleased to learn of it.'

Camille flushed indignantly. 'You would not have dared to speak to me like that in my father's time,' she answered, controlling herself with a visible effort.

Sorel shrugged his shoulders. '*Eh bien*, times have changed, they are always changing. Those papers prove nothing, and since they have been stolen I am no longer responsible for what they say. You have outwitted yourselves. Do your worst! You fools, the pair of you, you have bound Smith and myself together with hoops of iron! And what is your game, Collet?' he demanded, turning on Alf with a sudden snarl. 'You see, you have gained nothing at all. Why did you come here? A friend of Smith's, trying to play false with both sides, *hein?* No, no!' he shouted violently. 'I wish to God that I had never bought these lands, but now they are mine, not Smith's or anyone's, and no man or woman living shall take them from me. That is my final word. Go, mademoiselle! You, Collet, can get your money and leave my employment immediately!'

'Just a moment, Monsieur Sorel,' Alf intervened. 'We may as well be sure we've got all the facts clear, and then there won't be anything to regret afterward. You understand that Mademoiselle Destry is offering you terms that will give you a large share in the property, and that the question of her father's obligations to you, and yours to his, won't be brought up?'

'*Hein*, do I understand? You can't bluff me!'

'Another thing; you say I've bound Smith to you with hoops; well, he's aiming to cut those hoops mighty quick, Monsieur Sorel. It's you who're making the mistake. Are you sure that was your last word?'

Sorel did not reply, but remained facing him, glaring at him, one hand clenched, knuckles down, upon the table.

'And I guess I know what those hoops are, Monsieur Sorel,' Alf continued softly.

And as he spoke he was aware that Camille had flashed a sudden glance at him, and he intercepted it without turning his head. Alf would never have let her know of his suspicions of Sorel as the prime agent in her father's murder; but now, with an intuition so evanescent that it barely flashed into consciousness, a knowledge so fugitive that it had escaped him the next instant, leaving no trace, he knew that she suspected it, and that the expression upon her face, for some incomprehensible cause, was not horror but joy.

As for Sorel, he remained staring at Alf with a self-possession broken only by the tense, carven folds and lines of his white face, and the sudden horror in his blue eyes.

'*Damn him!*' he whispered through his clenched teeth. 'Collet, I'll talk to you alone.'

Alf shook his head.

'I'll talk to you alone,' snarled Sorel. 'Mademoiselle, you will oblige us — there is something I have to say to Collet.'

'Let him tell you, Monsieur Collet,' said Camille, turning to leave the room.

The moment she was gone, Sorel grasped Alf by the arm. 'What did you mean by that?' he whispered tensely. 'You make the bluff again, *hein?*'

'Not the least in the world.'

Sorel, glaring into Alf's face, saw that he knew, and Alf knew, in turn, that his suspicions were correct.

'It's a lie — but that does not matter. A lie can do a man as much harm as a truth. I guess you're playing for your own interests, Collet. Well, one can deal better with a rogue who is not a hypocrite as well. You are certainly a very intelligent man. *Eh bien*, Smith has got me in a corner. These conditions cannot go on much longer.'

'That's the truest thing you've said,' Alf answered. 'There's going to be bloodshed unless something breaks.'

'Am I a fool that I do not understand my own people? Do you think I have laboured all my life to get these lands in order to lose them — to lose them to the Yankee Smith? God in heaven, that man has hounded me! Since I first saw him there has been no peace. Damn him, the rogue, the cunning rat that has come nibbling, nibbling at me till he has eaten into me, eaten into my heart! Listen to me, Collet!'

He put his face close to Alf's and began whispering eagerly: 'Only one thing can save us all, but everything points to it. Everything is settled, there is a satisfactory compromise with Mademoiselle Destry, you become the foreman, the men return to their farms and their houses are rebuilt for them. Everything is adjusted, all are happy, for the poor man has a short memory. It is all forgotten. One thing: are you afraid? No one will ever know, and you and I are bound together forever. Dare you?'

Alf shook his head. 'I guess that skunk deserves to die about as well as any man I know, and that particular proposition's been put up to me before,' he answered, 'but I'm no murderer.'

'Pouf, *murder*!' Sorel's contempt was abysmal. 'Incite him to attack you. That will not be difficult. Then shoot. See, I will lend you a revolver. You keep it in your pocket. Insult him in the woods. Let him strike first. It is so easy. The Papineaus? If they suspect, they will be able to prove nothing, and they will not dare to move in the matter any way, there is too much against them. Are you a man, Collet?'

'Too much of a man for that.'

'Too much of a fool!' Sorel retorted

bitterly. 'Don't you see where our interests lie? What are you afraid of? Kill him like a man. Kill the dog!'

The door was flung wide open. Camille stood in the room again, with a white face and blazing eyes.

'He is right! *Kill him!*' she cried. 'Are you a *man*, Monsieur Collet? Do you not see? Kill him in fair fight, anyway, stab him in the back, shoot him while he is asleep, only kill him and set us all free!'

Alf looked at her stubbornly, defiantly, his lips compressed. Sorel peered into his face.

'Eh, mademoiselle, we have finished our talk, then!' he cried. 'It is useless, you see, it is altogether useless. *Eh bien*, it is all finished. Nothing more can be done. My answer to you is 'No!' '

He strode to the door and flung it wide. Alf followed him mechanically; and then he realised that the stage was already set as he had hoped and planned. For, it being Sunday, all the hands had assembled on the terrain in a rough semi-circle, their eyes fixed on the office. As Alf emerged there was a visible stirring among the group nearest, and then Pascal came forward and accosted him.

'Monsieur, you must go,' he stammered. 'Smith is waiting for you. He has told everybody — '

'Well?'

'That he intends to kill you, monsieur. You do not know his strength. He has sworn that he will kill you with his bare hands, Monsieur Collet. Ah, if only you had listened to me and Chamberland that day in the woods! Now there is no more to do but to leave quickly before he comes.'

As he spoke he kept glancing apprehensively toward the little bunkhouse, and now Alf could see that the eyes of all kept shifting between it and the mill. And suddenly Alf perceived the little storekeeper, Dubois, one of Egan's satellites, crossing the terrain in a slinking manner, evidently with the purpose of notifying his master of Alf's appearance.

Pascal's eyes, too, followed the man's movements. 'Be quick, monsieur,' he implored. 'There is nothing else to do We know you are with us, and we shall always be grateful to you.'

Sorel came up. 'Eh, Collet, I think you had better be gone,' he said. 'Smith has spoken of you. I cannot help you. Take my advice and go immediately.'

And suddenly, moved by an extraordinary impulse, he plunged his hand into his pocket, pulled out a wallet, and detached a twenty dollar bill. 'I'll arrange with Robitaille to take you to St. Joseph later,' he said hurriedly. 'You must hide till evening. Then come to my house. Run now!'

Alf looked from Sorel to Camille, who had come up, and stood watching him in hardly controlled agitation.

'What is it?' she breathed.

'I understand that Smith is proposing to carry out some of the threats he made to me last night,' said Alf. 'They want me to run away.'

'Yes, you must go,' pleaded Camille, her eyes wide with fear. 'You don't know the strength of that man. He has once stunned an ox with his fist, upon a wager. He will kill you — '

'Eh, with the bare hands, mademoiselle

— he has sworn it,' interposed Pascal.

'If you tell me to go,' said Alf slowly, 'I'll go, Camille.' He had never called her that before, but neither of them noticed the name. 'If I go, it means the end of — of everything. If you tell me to stay, I'll stay, and — and mebbe fight better. I've seen a lot of woods fighting. It isn't hopeless.'

'*He'll kill you!*'

Glancing across her shoulder, Alf now saw Egan coming out of the bunkhouse, attended by Alphonse Papineau. And the sight of that swaggering, lurching figure with the deformed shoulder aroused all his antipathies of the night before. Something primitive within him was trying to take control of him, his eyes swam, the lust for killing filled his body, tautened it to a tension of furious energy.

The men stirred, and Camille looked back and started, and looked at Alf again in wild appeal.

'You must go!'

'*Run!*' shouted Sorel, trying to thrust the bill into Alf's hand.

'I'd like you to tell me to stay,' said Alf to Camille.

And, as she stared at him in terror, she saw a light in his eyes that suddenly lit an answering light in hers.

'Stay, then,' she answered bravely. She flung her head back. She laughed. It was so defiant and brave a laugh, it rang out like a silver challenge. '*Stay*, Monsieur Collet,' she cried. 'I wouldn't have you do anything else.'

'Monsieur — Ah, monsieur — ' Pascal pleaded, tugging at Alf's arm.

If Alf had ever contemplated flight, it was too late. Egan was striding toward them. He wore a short white sweater, the sleeves rolled up above the elbow, displaying two forearms that were a mass of knotted muscles. As he advanced he shook his head from side to side in a tossing way, with something of the blind brutality of a wild ox, something at once gloating and confident, and totally impervious to the finer elements of that, or any situation.

As he drew near, the crowd fell back. An intense silence followed. Egan came up to Alf, looked at him — and passed him as if he had not noticed him. He walked up to Sorel and stood before him, his feet planted, the curve of his whole body expressive of the devilish mockery that animated him.

'Git out!' he snarled, with a contemptuous jerk of the thumb.

'Eh, monsieur, Monsieur Smith?' stammered Sorel.

'Git, I said. Your day's done, old man. I got no more use fer you. You git and don't you show your map on this property again.' He turned to the spectators, who, anticipating an attack on Alf, were struck dumb with surprise at this new development. 'Sorel's finished!' he shouted. 'His day's over. He's a damn thievin' swindler. These ain't his lands — they're Mademoiselle Camille's, and I got the papers provin' it. And I'm goin' to marry her. I'm your boss now — that's me, Smith.'

Sorel had grown purple. Confusion, anger struggled on his face. He stammered, flung his arms wildly about.

'You're lying!' he yelled. 'Come here,

you fool. I want to talk to you. Don't you see — '

'And if he shows his face on this property again, he'll be kicked out like a dog!' cried Egan. 'Me and Mademoiselle Camille's your bosses now, men,' he continued to the dumbfounded lumberjacks. 'Well, how about it, Sorel?' he continued, speaking more softly. 'You goin' quiet, or d'ya want me to tell jest how and why — '

Sorel stuttered incoherently, his arms revolved, he opened his mouth and tried to speak; then suddenly he pitched forward upon the turf at Egan's feet unconscious, his face suffused with blood, eyes horribly staring.

18

While Camille kneeled beside him, unfastening his coat and collar, Egan turned to Alf. He came up, his jaw thrust forward, his long arms hanging at his sides, his feet planted in the same stock-like manner. 'So you come!' he said in a soft, moaning whine. 'You come, Collet. I didn't look fer you. I'll hand it to you, you come.' He licked his lips. 'You come!' he repeated, as if his own words hypnotised him.

'I'll tell you what I'm going to do to you, Collet, you thievin' bum!' he shouted suddenly. 'Jest what I promised you last night. I'm goin' to break you with my hands. I'm goin' to hammer that pretty face of yours into a pulp, Alf Collet. I'm goin' to change you into a whinin', cringin' thing that your own mother won't reckernise. I'm goin' to teach you to butt in on other folk's affairs, you lying, thievin' jail-scum.'

213

Alf nodded his understanding.

But despite his resolution, his heart sank as he saw Egan's enormous strength. The man was built like a bull. Alf remembered that he had been the terror of the prize-ring, a foul hitter, grim, tenacious, murderous in his rage. Dimly he was aware of the circle of tense faces round them.

And suddenly these vanished. Consciousness of the spectators vanished. He saw nothing but Egan's face leering into his, and the knotted hands at Egan's sides. Then his momentary depression vanished in an uprush of abysmal fury.

The next instant, Egan had leaped forward from his standing posture, and driven both fists upward with two vicious, swinging blows aimed at Alf's chin. It was Egan's specialty, this upward chopping stroke, but it was a long time since he had used it, and Alf leaped backward just in time to foil a jar that would have rocked his nervous system. As Egan's arms shot up he broke through his guard with a smashing right to the chin that would have sent any ordinary man to sleep.

But Egan only recoiled and stood, shaking his head in surprise, as if momentarily dazed. Then he was coming on again, with the prize-fighter's crafty crouch, his long arms, with their extended reach, which made them terribly efficient weapons, held out in front of him, and the great knotted fists prepared to smash and hammer and batter their way to their objective.

It was years since Egan had been in the ring, and Alf could see that the brute strength of the man must have been at once his success and his limitation there. He had the cruder science of his trade, but beyond that there was little more than the brute to him. But Alf realised that his own science would serve him little, since he could not outmatch Egan in strength. For a few minutes he was puzzled, and stalled, backing away continually and studying his man. He saw the grin of self-confidence, which his blow had momentarily effaced, come back to Egan's face; and even while he hesitated he was nearly lost, for Egan possessed more agility than he had suspected, and

Egan's great fists suddenly broke through his guard, smashing in left and right, and knocking him to the ground.

In the moment of mental numbness that followed, Alf heard Camille's cry. Then he saw Egan's caulked boots, as if they filled the whole visible world, raised to stamp his face in. Then instinctively he had rolled out of reach, receiving only a painful, ripping shoulder kick, which began to spot his shirt with blood, found his feet, and confronting Egan again. His mouth was bleeding, and one eye was swelling, but now he stood up to the other and drove in. For a few moments the two stood breast to breast, hammering each other with terrific blows. But Egan received Alf's blows without a quiver, while each blow of Egan's felt like the impact of a steam hammer.

The lumberjacks, astounded that anyone could stand up to their master, had drawn closer, and gathered about the combatants in a circle. Alf was oblivious of them. He stood Egan's hammering until he realised that he was on the wrong tack, then broke away. His foot slipped, and a terrific right hook whirled him around. Next moment, however, as Egan came on with a bull's rush, Alf checked him with a pounding blow to the midriff that drew a gasp from him.

It was Egan's first sign of vulnerability. Alf had found his weak spot. It was like pounding an ox. For an instant Egan's great body seemed to suspend itself, as if impaled on Alf's fist. Then they had broken away, and Egan was coming on once more, craftily, planning a foul ending to the fight. He was losing his confidence. His slow mind could not understand how Alf could stand up under his attacks, and he could not work out his problem and fight at the same time; furthermore, having misjudged Alf's moral make-up, he was unable psychologically to reverse himself. Crouching, he sidled up like a great crab, and tried his upward blows again.

The slowness of his reactions gave Alf warning of what was coming. Egan's long reach again proved his weakness; and then a sudden wild yell sounded as Alf ran in with a quick right and left to the body and throat. Egan's head went back, the gross body went sprawling upon the ground.

Then the spectators swam back into Alf's ken once more, then Alf became aware of Camille standing among them, her hands locked in a fierce clasp of agitation. And with this he grew suddenly confident. He had tested Egan, and he found himself. He waited coolly as Egan struggled to his feet, astounded at not being kicked and battered while he was down. Egan came on, head down, bull-like, blood and saliva dripping from his cut lips. A stream of profanity broke from them.

Again Alf saw his chance. 'How about it?' he jeered. 'How about that hammering?'

'You scum!' bellowed Egan. 'I'm goin' to finish you now. I'm goin' to — '

Alf swung his head aside and let Egan's wild blow spend itself on the air. 'Listen, *Smith!*' he called, pronouncing the name tauntingly, 'I've got something to tell you — ' Avoiding the next infuriated rush, he added: '*I've* got those papers, not you. Get that into your thick head. The ones I gave you aren't worth the ink that's on them.'

He got it across, and for an instant Egan seemed paralysed by the realisation of it. He trembled; and then he came on with a fury that brooked no opposition. He clinched; and now Alf was no longer fighting Egan with fists opposed to fists, but fighting the whole weight of the gross form that held him, while Egan shot short, blinding jabs into his face. Instantly the blood was streaming down Alf's cheeks and lips. The furious body blows with which he sought to release himself made hardly any impression. Egan was literally hammering him into a pulp, as he had announced his intention of doing. His breath hissed into Alf's face, and there was once more supreme confidence in his eyes.

'I got ya now, ya jail scum!' he bellowed in Alf's ears.

And that, curiously, was the turning point. For in that struggle *will* counted for more than the difference in physical strength. Alf felt his whole personality in combat, all his past, and all that he had suffered in combat with the man who had sent him to the pen. He felt that, and it was that that nerved him to the supreme effort of summoning those super-physical reserves of strength which he had not quite depleted. He pulled himself together from the blackness that was gathering about him. Through it he saw his enemy's bloody face in a blood-stained leer above him.

He wrested himself free and took the offensive. He knew his time was short. It was all or nothing within one minute, perhaps — all the time he could last. He rained blow after blow on Egan's face and body. He drove the gross form backward. He gave it no time to recover between blow and blow. He was conscious of nothing but the supreme desire to crush this thing which was the cause of his ruined life. He fought like a madman under a whirling sky, in a ring of faces that went round and round, round and round, while the hoarse yells of the spectators filled the air with a volume of unmeaning noise.

And round and round went Egan, reeling under that battering rain of blows. The breath was hissing between his swollen purple lips, his leering face had changed into the hideous mask of a satyr, and the torrent of curses that had issued mechanically from between his lips had changed into sobbing imprecations.

Round and round Alf drove him. Egan stumbled, slipped, and crouched, shielding his head with his hands from the expected rain of kicks. But again Alf drew back, and Egan looked up at him with glassy eyes.

'Get up,' said Alf. 'I haven't finished with you yet!'

The yells had faded into silence. Egan looked in despair about him. But he was game. A bellow broke from his lips, a roar like that an ox gives after an ineffective blow with the pole-axe. He rose to his feet and stumbled forward, his arms whirling. Then Alf's right and left shot out and found their mark. Egan toppled and went down. And this time he did not rise or stir.

Alf, groping through the swimming

blackness, heard shouts of warning. A figure was leaping toward him. As it leaped he recognised, with an odd detachment of mind, Alphonse Papineau. He saw the knife in his hands. 'He's going to kill me,' he thought with a calmness that surprised him. 'This is the end.'

Then a second figure had leaped forward, seized Alphonse from behind, and flung him to the ground.

That was Chamberland. And suddenly the crowd, which had been held in a sort of equipoise of stupefaction, dissolved and rushed forward to where Egan still lay motionless, with glassy eyes staring up at the sky.

'*Kill* him!' they yelled. 'Death to the dog, the murderer, the burner!'

Alf straddled Egan's body. 'Leave him alone!' he mumbled thickly from between his swollen lips.

'No, monsieur, no!' They were forcing him backward. They were surrounding him, and dragging him away. But the blackness was dissolving. Alf found his voice.

'Listen, my friends,' he cried. 'All the

past ends here. But there must be no murder. Let this man go — and those!' He waved his hand toward the Papineaus, who, back to back, were snarling like wolves at the mob that surged about them. 'This land is Mademoiselle Destry's!' And then Alf found Camille. She was at his side, their hands were clasped, and she did not shrink from him, bloody and battered as he was.

'Will you work for her? Then listen to me! These lands that have been stolen from her are hers again. Drive these men off the property, but do not molest them. All the bad times are ended. You shall return to your farms and rebuild your homes. But let these men go.'

In the midst of the tumult that followed Alf called Pascal, Chamberland, and Robitaille, who were standing a few paces away.

'See that Smith and the Papineaus leave this land,' he said. 'But no harm must come to them. You understand, we shall lose everything if there is murder. From now on we work this land for mademoiselle. You understand?'

'*Oui, oui*, monsieur!'

'Then get a few of the older men around them and see that they are not harmed. As for Monsieur Sorel — ' His eyes lit upon Auguste Sorel, still lying where he had fallen. 'Is he dead?' he asked Camille.

'No, he is unconscious. I have given orders that he is to be taken home.'

Meanwhile the anger of the mob, which had been temporarily diverted by Alf's words, was again turning toward Egan. He was slowly struggling back to consciousness, and as he raised himself and looked about in dawning consciousness of what had happened to him, Pascal and Robitaille seized him, head and feet, and began carrying him away toward the edge of the terrain, where they laid him down beside the road. With them went the two Papineaus, hustled and jostled by the mob, which was, however, kept back by the efforts of a few of the more responsible men.

Alf and Camille found themselves momentarily alone. Camille looked up with swimming eyes into Alf's face. 'It is a wonderful victory,' she said. 'It is a miracle to me. I never dreamed it was possible. But it is not yet complete.'

'I know it,' answered Alf. 'But we've got him where we want him now, and there'll be no coming back. You — you remember — what I was telling you last night?' he continued, stammering.

'Yes,' answered Camille softly, 'I remember.'

'If I was to — '

But she checked him with a wistful look. 'When we are free, when we are sure that everything is past, you — you shall tell me again,' she said.

19

The first days that followed were a veritable revolution. Under Alf's management, the men took hold of the work with new energy and enthusiasm. An examination of the books showed that, as Alf had suspected, Egan's maneuvers had simply destroyed the efficiency of the company. It was in an admirable condition for being run at a profit. It had actually been run at a small loss. Alf resolved to make a success of it.

On the second day after the expulsion of Egan and the Papineaus, he announced his plans at a meeting. Standard wages were to be paid thenceforward, all the store debts were cancelled, new company houses for the workers and their families were projected, to take the place of the wretched shacks on the terrain, and, what gave the greatest satisfaction of all, the exiles at the Colony were invited to return to their farms and to reconstruct their homes with free lumber from the company's holdings.

Egan and the Papineaus had taken up their quarters at Dupont's groggery, from which comprehensive but vague threats emanated. As for Sorel, the apoplectic stroke which he had suffered had produced a partial paralysis. The old man had been left in the house that he had filched from Camille and her brother by her own wish. Sorel had lived there for years in Edouard Destry's time, and now Camille refused to let him be put out.

She herself had gone back to the log house, where she had decided to remain for the present. But for how long? Alf felt that she was the least optimistic of any of them. She seemed to regard the victory over Egan as only the initial round of the struggle which was still to be fought out. She was reticent with Alf, too, drawing back from him in a manner that baffled him.

He tried to remonstrate with her. 'Don't you see we've won?' he insisted. 'Everything belongs to you and your brother now. We've got the mill, and we can hold it. The only way Smith can put us out is by a successful lawsuit, and that's the last thing he'll dare undertake. And Sorel's finished.'

Sorel certainly was out of the running. The old man appeared to have relinquished himself to defeat. He lay all day in his chair, silent, attended by his housekeeper, brooding over the past.

But Alf could not bring the conviction that they had won home to Camille. Perhaps it was the problem of Philippe that contributed to her attitude. She knew that her brother was in some way involved with Egan. She knew that he still frequented Dupont's place nightly. He was more surly and even less communicative, and the effect of his constant drinking was showing in his puffed face and trembling limbs. The man seemed to be breaking down, and to have reached a point where the desire for liquor was ungovernable. He drank at home now, something he had not done before. And still Camille said not a word to him.

Alf tried to draw her out upon the subject of her brother, but she put him off with answers which meant nothing.

'There is nothing to be done. Philippe has always been like that,' she insisted.

'Do you think it possible that Smith has any hold over him?' Alf queried. 'It has occurred to me — ' He hesitated to suggest it, but went on. ' — perhaps he was in some way involved in that transaction over the lands.'

'No, Smith has no hold over him,' Camille answered, with a forced calmness that did not escape Alf. 'Only through drink; and he is debauching him because he knows — he knows that it is killing me!' she ended. And with a sob she was gone.

That was all Alf could gather. He could not understand why Camille kept him at arm's length, why the confidence between them seemed to have lapsed in the moment of victory. He felt that her attitude was reacting upon the men. She was playing into Egan's hands. And she met all his approaches with increasing coldness.

Two weeks had gone by since the fight, and still Egan remained at Dupont's and made no move. But from Dupont's sinister reports of his intentions began to trickle through. There Egan and the Papineaus were in touch with the lumberjacks, who frequented the place on Saturday nights and Sundays. In this respect Alf's action in raising their pay had proved disastrous. The years of slavery, the brutalities, even the burnings had been practically forgotten by these simple men with their passing. With the opening of the third week they returned to work in a different spirit.

Egan, Alf gathered, had treated them to a spree. Torrents of hooch had flowed, but no money had passed from the men to Dupont. The lumberjacks were sullen and jaded, a few of the younger men were mutinous. Alf determined to have a talk with Pascal upon the subject. He had put Pascal in charge of the carpenter's shop, where repairs had hitherto been made in a patchwork fashion by the elder Papineau. There had been continuous light falls of snow, the first severe frost would enable logging to be pursued with vigour, and the old man was busily at work with two assistants repairing the sleighs.

Alf drew Pascal aside and came straight to the point. 'Pascal,' he said, 'something's wrong with the men. Smith has been getting after them at Dupont's. I didn't think it possible that they could be such fools as to hanker after the old conditions again, but it rather begins to look that way to me. What does it mean?'

'Eh, monsieur, I had hoped that you would let me speak to you about that,' answered Pascal. 'It is unfortunate, monsieur. You see, they are like children, our people — now up, now down.' He made a see-saw movement of his hands.

'Yes — well, what has sent them down again? Don't they realise how much better off they are than when they were under Smith and Sorel? Do they want to get the old days back again or don't they? Do they expect to get their wages increased once more if Smith comes back?' he continued in bitter sarcasm. 'Can't they see where their own interests lie, to say nothing of gratitude?'

'Assuredly they see, monsieur,' Pascal answered with a little hesitation. 'And

231

they are grateful to you, monsieur. But they say that you are not one of us. They say that the Yankee is here today and gone tomorrow.'

'So that's the line Smith's been taking with them, is it?'

Pascal shrugged his shoulders in a deprecating manner. 'They say you mean well, monsieur, only you do not understand. And Smith tells them all the time that in only a little while he comes back, and then all who have been faithful to him will be rewarded. The men do not know what to think. And there is much liquor going at Dupont's.'

'Well, what's to be done?'

Pascal went on in his hesitating way: 'You see, monsieur, what the men are saying is that they thought it was for Mademoiselle Destry that they were now working, and mademoiselle hardly ever comes to the mill now — '

'I understand,' said Alf. 'So they think I can't hold down this job for her?'

'And Smith has spread it everywhere that she is to marry him, and she — she does not come here and so show that the story is false. Ah, monsieur, if you could persuade her to show the men that she is the master, and that you are working for her — '

Alf nodded. 'I'll have a talk with her, Pascal, and we'll send that lying story back where it belongs. But by the way, how do the men imagine that Smith is going to get the mill back?'

Pascal hesitated for a long while. 'I do not believe it, monsieur,' he said at last, 'but it is reported that he has sent to Montreal for the sheriff and his deputies.'

Alf laughed. 'There won't be anything doing along that line, Pascal,' he answered. 'You can tell the men that from me. And I'm going to see Mademoiselle Destry and put the situation before her.'

He said nothing to Camille about Pascal's story of the sheriff, in which he put not the slightest credence, and, of course, nothing about Egan's circulated lie regarding herself and him, but he tried to outline the conditions as forcibly as possible, refusing to let himself be put off.

'It's this way, as far as I see it,' he

summarised. 'We can't put Smith and the Papineaus out of the district. They're hanging on at Dupont's, and they're gradually corrupting your men with their free liquor. As a body the men are loyal. But they aren't loyal to me. They're loyal to you. You've got to work on that instinct in them, or it's only a matter of a little time before Smith will corrupt enough of them to enable him to venture on something — something that will put the mill back in his hands. Won't you let them see that you are their boss?'

'What do you want me to do?'

'Go back to your home. Do what you like with Sorel, but go back. Let the men understand that this is Destry land again, and that you are the owner.'

'And Philippe?'

Something in the question, perhaps the hopelessness of the tone, chilled Alf. And they looked at each other in silence, each absorbed in his own unspoken question.'

Alf put his first: 'Won't you be frank with me, Camille? Why should Philippe come between us now?'

And then Camille put hers: 'And you,'

she said, 'will you not tell me why you came up here, and why you needed Sorel's papers?'

There was a longer pause. 'I can't tell you,' answered Alf.

'Nor can I,' Camille retorted.

Alf tried once more. He took her by the hands. 'Camille, won't you try to look at it this way? We've put this thing through by working together. We must go on. If there is something neither of us can speak about to the other just now — ought that to be allowed to break up our under-standing? You've at last won what you've been trying to get back — your lands and your position. And if you'll only take the lead the men will be loyal to you. Are you going to throw everything away? It isn't asking much. If you won't take the lead, how can the men be blamed for falling under Smith's influence again?'

She seemed moved for a moment, then she drew back into herself in the way Alf was coming to know so well. 'You don't understand,' she answered. 'There's no use talking about it   there's nothing I can do. I've thought that perhaps if you told me why you had come here, things might have been different. But I don't care now!' she cried, startling Alf with the sudden tragic intensity of her demeanour. 'You don't know how much my brother means to me. I'd give my life for him. I remember how fond we were of each other when we were children. He was good then, and he's good now. He's honourable at heart. People don't change when they grow up. If he were not good I wouldn't care.

'I'd give back the mill to Smith or to Sorel, or anyone who'd see that the men were not turned off their farms, and that they were paid a fair rate of wages. And I'd take Philippe and we'd go somewhere where no one would know us and no one ever find us. Only he'd follow me — that man. He told me he had never in his life failed to get what he wanted, and he means to make me marry him. Don't speak to me about this again.'

She drew her hands violently out of Alf's, and put them over her face, shuddering.

'Camille, promise me that you won't marry him!'

'Never — *never!*' she cried.

'It isn't hopeless, then?' Alf was speaking of himself now. 'Camille, I've as good as told you what you know, about — about the way I feel. I guess I've got no right — but you know, anyway, and if there was any chance I'd wait forever.'

'You talk of love,' she answered bitterly, 'and you don't trust me!'

'Someday — when the time comes — I'll tell you everything, Camille.'

'Then that's my answer too!' she cried. 'How can there be love without faith and confidence? That's all I have to say till — till that 'someday' of yours arrives!'

20

On the day after his fight with Egan, Alf
had approached Camille upon the subject
of finding a refuge for Celeste Trudeau.
He had no doubt but that Camille would
immediately offer to accommodate her in
the colony. He had been chilled and
astonished by the coldness with which
Camille had received his suggestion. He
was not sufficiently versed in life to know
that even the gentlest and most unselfish
of women feel toward such women as
Celeste an ineradicable hostility which
they find it impossible to conceal. Alf had
pleaded Celeste's cause more warmly,
and Camille had only grown the cooler.
At last Alf had to satisfy himself with
Camille's assurance that she would think
the matter over and see what could be
done.

And Alf had not the smallest idea how
heavily this trivial incident weighed in the
scale of Camille's mind. A woman in the

beginnings of love is a creature of moods, whims, impulses, of quick denials of her heart. The mere fact that Alf was concerned about another woman, however innocently, and however impossible disloyalty to her appeared, seemed to Camille an affront that required a world of expiation.

This was only a factor in her change of attitude, and a small one, but it was the one that turned the scale, made her withhold her confidence, and so reversed the entire situation.

Realising that Camille would do nothing to help Celeste, Alf became obsessed by the idea that she would kill herself. He wanted to see her and talk over his plans for her, but he had drawn no money since his arrival, and he was penniless. He did not know what to do. He decided that the best thing would be to persuade her to hold out till his first payday, and then to induce her to let him give her the fare to Montreal.

On the first available evening, he set out for her shack with this object in view. When he came in sight of Dupont's, he left the trail and circled through the trees, with the purpose of reaching her room unobserved. But he soon perceived that the little candlelight in the groggery came from the attic overhead in which the man and his sons slept; the saloon was dark, for it was a week day, and it was only at weekends Dupont kept open house.

Two of the cubicles were dark as well. The female 'boarders' had gone back to Montreal, enriched by the spoils gleaned from their admirers, in spite of Dupont's urgings and promises. But in the cubicle at the end there shone the light of a little lamp. By it Alf could see Celeste seated in a low rocker, rocking to and fro. Her hands were folded on her lap, and it seemed to Alf that he had never seen such a hopeless look on any human face before.

For a moment or two he could not bring himself to intrude on it. Then, just as he was about to approach the door, he fancied he heard someone stirring in the underbrush at the edge of the forest. He stopped and listened, but the sound was not repeated, and, going up to the door, he knocked softly.

At the sound Celeste sprang to her feet, her face tense with expectation. She opened the door and stood staring at Alf with sudden hope in her eyes, as if she thought that he had somehow in his hands the gift of happiness for her. Then the look died away, and was succeeded by one of apathy.

'I couldn't fix it, about getting you a place to live,' said Alf. 'Not yet, but I'm still trying. I'm going to do everything I can. Can you hold out a little longer?'

Celeste's hands were groping for support. Alf caught her in his arms as she swayed. 'I — thought it was — somebody else,' she whispered faintly. 'I didn't know you at first, Monsieur Collet.'

Suddenly, as he was about to release her, she seemed to stiffen. She screamed, and Alf saw her eyes dilate with terror as she stared over his shoulder. Next moment a figure had leaped at Alf from behind. It was only Alf's instinctive movement that saved him from the long knife which glanced over his shoulder, clutched in a sinewy hand whose violent

241

impact sent Alf reeling.

For just that instant Alf saw the hand and the knife — no more. He had just time to seize the wrist when the impact sent them both crashing against the little table, upsetting the lamp. It crashed to the floor and went out in a tinkle of broken glass. And then Alf found himself wrestling for life with his assailant.

There was only one assailant, and in a few seconds Alf knew that he was neither Egan nor one of the Papineaus. He was smaller, much smaller than either of that pair, and weaker, though he was fighting with devilish fury. It was all Alf could do to retain his hold upon the wrist and keep the point of the knife averted from him. But in a few moments more the man's energy seemed to exhaust itself. Alf succeeded in twisting the wrist in such a manner as to send the knife flying across the floor. He got the man underneath him, his hands upon his throat. The frenzied struggles began to weaken.

'Get a match — light a candle!' Alf called to Celeste, who was crouching in a corner, sobbing hysterically from fear.

'It's all right now. Get a light and we'll see who this fellow is. I'm holding him.'

But though subdued the man's spirit was not conquered. He writhed and wrestled impotently in Alf's grasp, and each time Alf relaxed his hold upon his throat a trifle a volley of imprecations broke from his lips. It seemed an eternity before Celeste had struck a match, with shaking fingers that had already failed to ignite several, and managed to apply the flame to the wick of a candle-end. Alf peered into the man's face.

'Now, my unknown friend,' he said, 'let's have your business prompt and to the point.'

The other only snarled wickedly. And as the flame shot up Alf discovered that this was no man from St. Laurent — at least none that he had ever seen. And yet he had seen him somewhere. He let his mind grope back. And then he knew him.

It was the little rat, the last of the runaway gang who had come up with him, and whom he had kicked off the platform of the station at St. Joseph.

As the man staggered sullenly to his

feet Celeste recognised him, too. '*Charles!*' she cried wildly.

'Yes, it's *me*,' growled the other, looking shiftily at Alf, as if he meant to renew the assault, but realised its futility without the knife, at which he glanced in the corner where it lay. 'Ah, infamous woman, what have you to say! Night after night this week past I have watched at your window to see who your lover is. Ah, you were crafty in concealing him, but I swore to kill him when I knew. And I'll kill you, I swear to kill you!' he snarled at Alf.

'Charles, you are wrong, you are wrong. Monsieur Collet — '

But the name seemed to arouse the rat to a paroxysm of fresh fury.

'The *name!*' he shouted. 'That is the name Alphonse gave to me, my good friend Alphonse Papineau, whom I trusted, the only man who knows I'm here. I wouldn't trust that man, Egan, but I trusted Alphonse, and he was true to me. Eh, do you intend to marry?' he grimaced.

Celeste ran forward and caught him by

the arm, clinging to him as he tried to force her away. 'Charles, you shall listen!'

'Listen to lies? *Maudit*, why should I listen to them? You were betrothed to me, and when I dared not return you wrote that you would be true to me. I believed you, and many times I started to come home, and once I reached St. Joseph with a gang of men, but all the rest had run away, and I dared not come alone. Now, a week ago, I come. I hide in the woods, in a cave, like an animal, seeing none but my good friend, Alphonse Papineau. 'Is she well?' I ask him. '*Ma foi oui*, the most faithful of women — to the Yankee Collet, our new master. Kill him, Bartel; I shall not know anything about it.''

'Charles, he was lying to you. Monsieur Collet isn't the man. He has been kind to me. He came tonight to help me. I swear Alphonse Papineau lied. I swear it, Charles!'

So vehement was her denial that for the first time Charles Bartel began to waver. His shifty look became uncertainty. He passed his hand over his forehead. Suddenly he began sobbing.

245

'I don't know what to believe. All lies!' he wept. 'Celeste, thou knowest that I loved thee. I was in trouble, in danger, and I dared not return because they knew where my home was, and Egan told me he would see that you came to no harm. But at last I became desperate at hearing nothing. So I came, and — but there has been another man!' he cried.

He read the answer in Celeste's averted face. Murder gleamed in his eyes. He glared about him like a beast that is trapped. Celeste still clung to him.

'Charles, forgive me! He told me that you had another woman and that you would never return. He made me love him. He deceived me. Now he is tired of me. Charles, you shall let me speak!' she cried, clinging the tighter as he tried with all his might to shake her from him. 'Only Monsieur Collet here has helped me. All the men mocked me, and the women, too. I should have killed myself but for Monsieur Collet. Charles, if you can forgive, take me away; if you can't, take me still and let me be your servant. I am going mad here, mad with the waiting, desperate . . . '

Alf turned away. Celeste was on her knees, beseeching him. Charles Bartel stood there, shaken by his irresolution.

'Celeste,' he said at last, 'it is hard. It is the hardest thing in the world. I never dreamed this could happen to you. If I forgive and take you away, I must know who the man is. Not Egan?' The sudden suspicion lit up his face with new frenzy.

'Egan? I do not know him,' answered Celeste with obvious sincerity.

'Who, then?'

What will you do, Charles?'

'Kill him!'

'I will not tell.'

'Then — ' He flung her from him.

Celeste ran back to him. 'All right, I'll tell you,' she babbled, 'but there must be no killing. It was Monsieur Smith.'

Charles Bartel looked at her in bewilderment. 'Smith? An American? I do not know him. Where is he, then?'

'I don't know,' lied Celeste, grasping at her new opportunity. 'He is gone away.'

'Where is he gone?'

'I don't know, Charles. He has gone

away forever. He was discharged and has gone back to Montreal. Take me, Charles.'

'When I return.'

'When will that be?'

'Soon, Celeste. In two or three nights. No one must know that I have returned. I'll take you through the forests, that way I came. *Hein!*' The look of cloudy craft came into his eyes again. 'This Smith told you I had another woman. He knew me, then? Or did he lie?'

Celeste started. 'Listen!' she cried in a sibilant whisper.

In the darkness outside they heard the sound of footsteps coming up the trail. In a moment, like a lithe shadow, Charles Bartel had slipped out of the hut and disappeared among the trees.

As Alf turned away, conscious that his mission was ended, Dupont came up and stood wagging his red beard at him. 'Eh, a wet night, monsieur,' he chuckled, pointing to the falling snow. 'A bad night for visiting, monsieur.' His eyes roamed from Alf to Celeste, and he chuckled again.

Alf nodded curtly and strode homeward. He was glad the burden of Celeste was off his mind. But his own problem was no easier.

21

To Camille, Alf's victory over Smith had
been only the opening of the struggle. To
her, the contest revolved much more
around herself than about the possession
of the lands and the mill. Until the
personal menace of Smith was removed
from her, she could not concentrate upon
what was, for her, the lesser detail. She
dreaded and feared the man, his power,
his personality, which fascinated her as a
snake might; his influence over Philippe.
It was that feeling that Alf had achieved
only the lesser victory, while the greater
was as far as ever away, that was the
beginning of the estrangement.

Then there was the matter of Celeste
that weighed so heavily. Camille could
not understand how Alf could interest
himself in a woman of that type. To her
such women were less than human, she
allowed them hardly human rights. And
this was less self-righteousness than a

profound realisation of their influence over the lumberjacks who came under their sway. One of her earliest recollections was of seeing a drunken dance in a saloon run by a predecessor of Dupont, when as a child she had stolen out of the house and wandered up the trail. The sight had sickened her, without her understanding it, and it had perhaps worked in her unconsciously, to emerge quickened when Alf preferred his request to her.

But this was only the deciding factor. For now that nebulous phantom in her mind, which she had beaten back from the borderland of consciousness again and again — that dark spot which she had always shunned began to be illuminated once more. And she could no longer stem the slow approach of that terror which was creeping upon her, like an uplifted arm that would someday fall and strike her down.

Because she knew she loved Alf, she was the more beset by her fears. Who was he, and why was he at St. Laurent? Why had he wanted Sorel's papers? His refusal to satisfy her both piqued and frightened her, and she had traced in her mind a fantastic connection between his presence there and the revival of her fears. And his obstinacy awoke an answering obstinacy in herself, and doubts of him. When he was with her she believed in him and trusted him, but in his absence those doubts awakened. And in her despair the plan grew more and more insistently in her mind to escape with Philippe from St. Laurent and never return.

But how was she to broach the subject to her brother? Despite his occasional fantastic assumption of dignity, as the *soi-disant* seigneur, the man seemed lost to all sense of shame now. Liquor had apparently become the sole purpose of his existence. Before their father's death, though he had been dissolute, he had been high-spirited, not lost to all self-respect. And by the terms of the unspoken understanding between them they were to go their own ways. Pride held her from making an appeal to him.

But it was Philippe who opened the

door between them. He had come home one night less drunk than usual. He flung himself down in a chair, apparently brooding over something. Camille grew more and more uneasy under his persistent scrutiny. At last she raised her head in embarrassment.

'Well, what is it, Philippe?' she asked. 'Why are you staring at me?'

'That Yankee, that man Collet, he doesn't come here anymore. Does he think he has inherited our lands now? Or do you two no longer intend to marry?'

Camille rose up indignantly. 'Philippe, how dare you suggest that — '

But she stopped in confusion, and Philippe sniggered. 'Do you think, then, that everybody else in St. Laurent is blind?' he demanded. 'Is not everyone asking the same question? I am your brother, but it is difficult for me to protect your reputation when it is being said everywhere that the Yankee has jilted you.'

'I don't think, Philippe,' answered Camille bitterly, 'that you have ever had my reputation very seriously at heart. But enough of this. You are forgetting the understanding between us.'

'Understanding? I tell you I've had *enough* of this sort of *understanding*!' cried Philippe, springing to his feet and confronting his sister with a sudden outburst of rage. 'This cannot go on. Well? What have you to say? I am not a *child*, that I should be shut out of everything. We have antagonised Monsieur Smith, our friend, after he had put Sorel off our lands and regained them for us, and now the Yankee has stepped in. That has been our mistake.'

'*Your* mistake, Philippe, was in letting Smith buy your liquor for you,' said Camille icily. 'You have placed yourself under obligations to him; I do not know how far you have committed yourself, but if you think I shall ever accept his terms — you know what they are,' she continued in deep agitation. 'If you think I shall ever become his wife — '

'Listen, Camille. I — I have been thinking it over. We are Destrys, we have our pride and our traditions, but after all times have changed, and the man Smith is at least no worse than that other man, Collet — '

But he could not meet the eyes of blazing anger that Camille turned on him. 'So has sent you to me as his go-between, his *marriage broker*!' she cried.

'No, no, Camille,' Philippe put in hastily. 'Of course, if you are unwilling — and it would be beneath you, I should hardly hold up my head. But the lands — the lands . . . we cannot live forever in this way. I am the seigneur — '

'Well, well, you are the *seigneur*, as you say, Philippe,' retorted Camille in biting mockery. 'And what then? What is all this conversation about?'

'What is that Yankee doing at our mill? What are you doing? That is what everybody is asking!' cried Philippe. 'Now that Auguste Sorel is finished, Monsieur Smith is willing to make fair terms with us. And you — you do nothing. Neither hot nor cold. That is what it is so difficult to understand. Why do you not come to terms with him? He is our good friend. I am farseeing, and it was not for nothing that I remained his friend. I knew how to keep silent, but I was not working in the dark. It was Sorel who was our enemy, not Monsieur Smith.

'Now listen,' he continued excitedly. 'While he thought that he was using me, I was taking his measure. What is to prevent our putting the Yankee Collet off the lands and coming to terms with Smith? Let him think that you will marry him, and then repudiate the agreement. Laugh at him. That is the privilege of women. You should see the women in Montreal! Make a fool of him! Have you no sense, Camille? Any other woman would have thought of that long ago. Marriage — no, only in the last resort, if we become destitute, but — trick him, trick him! What is the use of being a woman if you will not avail yourself of your powers?'

She looked contemptuously at the drunkard; at such moments her love for Philippe and her loathing for the thing he had become gave him the aspect of two entities in her mind. She knew that Smith would never abandon his intention of making her his wife. What was behind this move? That was the sole thing that concerned her. How far was Philippe taking this course out of selfishness, and how far was Smith driving him?

'You — you are the seigneur, you tell me,' Camille said unsteadily, 'and yet you come to me with so base a proposition as this, Philippe!'

He hung his head; even to his drink-sodden mind the baseness of his suggestion was beginning to penetrate.

'But it is for the lands,' he blustered. 'There is good money in them. And it is all for your sake. I only think of you. I would be content to sell my share for a very small sum, a few thousand dollars, perhaps, and then I would go to Montreal and start a business there.'

A spasm of pity for him pierced Camille's heart. She put out her hand and clasped his. 'Philippe,' she said gravely, 'how would you like to come away from St. Laurent with me?'

'To Montreal?' he demanded eagerly.

'No, farther than Montreal. To some

western city, perhaps, where we need never think of this place, or of all our troubles.'

To her surprise, he leaped at the suggestion. 'I should like nothing better,' he answered eagerly. 'And, leave everything. Leave Smith and the Yankee to fight it out together. It is a fine idea!' It ran to his head like liquor. 'And first Monsieur Smith will pay us a good sum for giving up our rights.'

'No — without any money, Philippe.'

His face fell. 'When?' he stammered.

'I — I don't know yet, Philippe.'

He looked at her with a flash of intuition. 'Ah, it is the Yankee Collet,' he sneered. 'You have quarreled with him. And I was forgetting to tell you. You are not the only one. Do you begin to understand now, Camille? There is a woman at Dupont's, by name Celeste Trudeau. He used to visit her even when he was our guest, when he was making love to you — '

'That is *enough*, Philippe!' cried Camille fiercely. 'When you have reached the point where you insult me, you are no longer my brother. You or I will leave this house — '

But she was unable to conceal her agitation, remembering as she did that it was from Alf's lips that she had last heard the name of Celeste Trudeau.

Philippe caught at her arm. 'I can prove it to you!' he cried. 'Tonight he goes to see her, as he goes every night. Come with me, and you shall find them together. You must come with me, Camille. You are my sister. I must protect you against this Yankee who tricks and deceives you.'

She looked at him in terror. Philippe's eyes gleamed with craft. She hated her brother at that moment. She felt that the last bond between them was broken. And yet until she knew that he was lying to her her mind would never be at peace again.

'Camille, he has deceived you. He is nothing but a jailbird, who has fled up here to escape imprisonment. He admitted it to Smith. Come with me. It is only to look — to see him there with her. No one need know that we have been there. Then you will see the truth. And you will believe the truth, eh, sister?'

'I shall believe — the truth. But it is a lie!' answered Camille uncertainly.

'It is no lie, my poor sister. And then you will order him to leave our property, eh, sister?' Philippe continued confidently. 'No, it is no lie. I only ask that you come with me.'

'I'll go with you, then. I'll go with you to prove that it is a lie!' cried Camille.

22

The futile interview with Camille left Alf baffled and bewildered. Egan was winning, by the slow momentum of time and change. Something must be done. But what? For the first time since his arrival at St. Laurent Alf abandoned himself to despair.

He had come within an ace of success, only to be beaten back by some intangible factor. He had failed in his efforts to discover Destry's murderer, he had failed in his endeavour to reinstate Camille and her brother as owners of the seigniory. There was no further passage the way he had chosen. He must retrace his steps. But how far back?

Looking at the matter, it was impossible to avoid the conclusion that Camille was turning away from him. Inexplicable as it was, there was no other conclusion. She had been turning from him ever since the fight with Egan. She had abandoned

261

him in the moment of victory. And everything was fast slipping out of their grasp.

He had exhausted every effort to induce her to back his management of the property, so that he could push home the victory, and she had met him upon personal grounds. There was nothing more to be done along the lines he had followed. The only thing left for him was to meet her own conditions.

Unless a reconciliation could be effected, he would have to leave the mill. But Camille herself had laid down the conditions of reconciliation. If he would tell her why he had come to St. Laurent their friendship and alliance would be restored. Alf knew he had one card left to play. He had played it before, and failed, but for all that it was the last card in his pack — Sorel. Sorel had refused terms, but that was when he was master of the lands and the mill. It might be very different now.

Sorel alone could clear up the mystery of the murder and put in Camille's hands the proofs of the ownership of the lands.

Report had it that he was dying. Would he, out of hatred of Egan, or from the simple wish to right a wrong, provide the clue to the situation?

It seemed the only chance remaining. Accordingly, the following afternoon Alf made his way up the hill to Sorel's house.

He did not enter by the front door, but walked round to the little back room, and, looking in, saw that it had been converted into a bedroom. Sorel was stretched out in a long chair beside his desk, which was littered with papers. He seemed to have been writing, but now he sat listlessly in his chair, his paralysed left arm hanging at his side, and his left leg propped up on the extended foot-rest. Alf was shocked at the change in the man. Sorel seemed to have aged fifteen years during the two weeks that had passed; his hair was entirely white.

As Alf stood outside, looking in, Sorel turned his china-blue eyes upon him. Those eyes alone seemed to reflect something of the old vigour of the man. Without starting or betraying any emotion, as if he had known that he was there, Sorel beckoned to Alf to enter.

Alf raised the sash and leaped inside the room. He stood before the old man, and for a little while they surveyed each other in silence.

'*Eh bien*, I told you you were a fool, Collet,' said Sorel. 'You could have been much, very much at St. Laurent. What are you now? The manager for the Destrys? Pouf!'

The indescribable gesture of contempt that he made told Alf that, from some source or other, Sorel knew everything, or, at least, that he had shrewdly summed up developments.

'See what you have lost, Collet. If you had been loyal to me you would have found much to your advantage. I said to you when first you came here that I could use a man whom I could trust, did I not — *hein?*' The china-blue eyes bored into Alf's with an inscrutable expression.

'I guess that's so, Monsieur Sorel,' admitted Alf. 'But I was playing my own hand. I guess you'll understand that; you've always played yours.'

'*Ben, ben*,' replied Sorel quickly. 'So we

understand each other. But this hand of yours — it has been a poor hand, eh, Collet?' He swung round sharply in his chair. 'Listen, now, Collet, and I will explain to you my life and my motives. It would be a good thing to be understood by one person, and I have taken a liking to you, Collet. It is very unfortunate that you would not kill Smith, who tried to kill you, but then you did not understand. You were like the bull in the shop of china, blundering in here — *hein?*

'I was growing old, Collet, and I found the possession of these lands less satisfying than I had thought. *Diable*, it is a strange thing, but as soon as a man gets what he has always wanted he is no longer satisfied with it. From the time when I was a boy I wanted the Destry lands, especially when I saw what a fool old Monsieur Destry was, and how they were slipping away from him. If it had not been me it would have been somebody else who would have taken them away from him. I was going to do big things when I became the seigneur. And I was going to marry and have a son who should inherit

265

after me, but by the time the lands came to me it was too late.

'You Americans are not like us; you are not burdened with that loyalty which is — how do you say it? — the soul of a man, his very nature, as we *Canayens* are. For I tell you, Collet, I am a loyal man at heart, and if Monsieur Edouard had not been such a fool I should have continued to serve him faithfully.

'If he could have held his lands — but he could not. It was always money, money, and he was draining himself dry. Do you understand how the peasant looks on his little plot of earth, Collet; that it is his life, his soul, that he loves it more than his wife and children, his animals? *Eh bien*; that is the loyalty of the *habitant* to his land, and that is my loyalty to the Destry land. That is why I have held these lands — for Mademoiselle Destry. Do you begin to understand?

'Because Monsieur Philippe is heir under the law, and because he would have squandered them even more quickly than his father — that is why I have held these lands, so that they shall pass to mademoiselle under my will. Eh, you are beginning to see the light now? You see now why I wanted a loyal man to work with me, *hein*, Collet? And you have — how do you say it? — queered the game by blundering in, and yet you are not man enough to kill Smith. Now he wins.'

'He needn't win,' said Alf doggedly. 'That's what I came to see you about, Monsieur Sorel. But first I'm going to tell you something. I guess I did make a mistake, although I don't quite see how, and I wanted to stand in with you all along, only things didn't turn out that way. However, I'm going to put my cards on the table. I'm going to tell you why I came up here. You were pretty close to it when you thought I was hiding. I was. I've been hiding for years, and I'm sick of hiding. I want to look the world in the face again. I heard Smith was up here. I used to know him under the name of Egan. When I was a kid he roped me into crooked ways in Fall City — '

There was not a flicker in Sorel's china-blue eyes, not the vestige of an expression on his face.

'So far as I understand, he'd arranged to have an old man killed, and I was to be the decoy duck. I was to be pinched for it, and then go to the gallows. Well, they got me. Only I got off with a life sentence. That old man was Edouard Destry.'

Sorel's expression was absolutely mask-like.

'I escaped from the pen and came up here to find this Egan under the name of Smith. I guessed he wouldn't recognise me, and he didn't. I've been trying to clear myself, find out who it was murdered Destry, so that I can go back into the world and hold my head up again. That's why I broke into this house that night and stole your papers, though it was Smith proposed it to me. His game was to find that Camille Destry owned the land, and then to put you off and marry her. Mine was to find out the name of Destry's murderer.

'All that's not entirely news to you. But now I'm putting this straight. You hired Egan to murder Destry. That's blunt, but it's to the point. It's true. You're as good as his murderer.'

He paused to let Sorel speak, but he might as well have paused for a statue. The only sign of emotion in Sorel was a slight involuntary twitching of the muscles about his lips. Alf went on after a moment or two: 'Well, that's how Egan got his hold over you. That's why he's been running this place and making you play second fiddle until he got ready to put you out. But he's overplayed his hand now. He can't denounce you without denouncing himself. And if I size you up correctly, Monsieur Sorel, you've never committed yourself to that murder plot in writing. You see I'm talking to you straight.

'Well — Egan's overplayed his hand. He doesn't own a rood of land here. If what you said is true, and Camille Destry's going to get the land in your will, clean up this business and put Smith off the limits. And if you've been lying to me, and her brother's the owner under the law, clean it up just the same, and put an end to Smith. Nobody can clean up this business but you.'

269

Sorel spoke for the first time. 'And where do you come in, Collet?' he sneered malevolently.

'*Me?*' retorted Alf violently. 'Why, I'm not asking favours from you, unless you choose to tell me who it was that did the killing, so that I can go to Mademoiselle Destry and tell her why I came to St. Laurent, and that I'm no murderer. But there's no reason why you should do that for me.'

Suddenly the mask-like immobility of Sorel's features seemed to dissolve. 'You — you Collet,' he said derisively, 'you *blunderer*, there are things that you will *never* understand. Do you think that *I*, Auguste Sorel, should have permitted myself to be put off my own lands by that usurper Smith if there were not very excellent reasons for it? And you do not understand so much, do you?' he sneered. 'You do not understand what Smith is doing here, or what he hopes for, or why Mademoiselle Camille is no longer your friend, *hein*, Collet?

'But I will do one thing for you, because I like you, Collet. I'll tell you who

270

killed Edouard Destry: I did it. Perhaps you begin to see now why I cannot oppose this fellow Smith, *hein*, Collet? Edouard Destry had a large sum of money with him, part of the price I had paid him for his lands. Smith — yes, Egan, he called himself — agreed to have Monsieur Edouard killed, and he was to have one-third of the money. But then he backed out. The men whom he had hired refused to commit the murder at the last moment. I was desperate. I had borrowed that money and I had to have it. So I waylaid Monsieur Destry, and *I* struck him on the head with an iron bar, and killed him, like any murderer of a city slum. Now do you understand? Are you satisfied now, *hein*, Collet?' he cried triumphantly. 'That is between us two, but for the world outside, if you repeat that story, you are lying, and who will believe you?' Sorel swung back in his chair. 'My advice to you is to *go*,' he said. 'Be warned, Collet, and leave St. Laurent without delay. You can do nothing. That is my last word to you.'

23

Sitting in his shack that evening, trying to sort out the strands of the tangled situation, Alf felt that Sorel's malicious confession of the murder was the most inexplicable part of all that had happened.

Alf had looked forward so eagerly to the day when he should confront the murderer and wrest the truth from him; he had never dreamed that Sorel's hands had wielded the implement that had crushed in Destry's skull.

And why had he confessed to him? A priest would have relieved his conscience and buried the secret deep.

He had confessed out of simple malice, it seemed to Alf, malice of the same kind as that he had shown when the huts of the peasantry were scheduled for burning. He was no weakling. No impulse had prompted him to tell Alf that story. And it was quite clear now that nothing was to be done. Alf's road had simply led him up against a blank wall.

He must abandon his task as hopeless and leave St. Laurent. He would not make another appeal to Camille. His judgment over-rode the desperate impulse to try once more. He would leave St. Laurent as speedily as possible.

Alf was just reaching this conclusion when there came a tap at the door, and a red-haired shifty-eyed lad came in and stood leering at him in the entrance. Alf recognised the boy as Dupont's younger son, who worked about the groggery, and had already an intimate knowledge of the baser side of life, as it was demonstrated to him. There was the hint of an understanding in the furtive, impudent glance that the lad shot at Alf.

'Well?' Alf demanded.

'Monsieur Collet, she has sent me for you. She wishes to speak to you,' said Dupont's son with a grin.

'Who?' Alf's first thought was that he came from Camille; that she was in need of him.

'Celeste Trudeau. She says it is very

important that you should come to her immediately, monsieur.'

The idea instantly flashed into Alf's mind that Egan might be setting a trap for him. But almost as quickly he reassured himself. Egan would hardly be likely to try the crude game of murder at the present juncture.

'All right; tell her I'll come,' Alf answered.

When the boy was gone he went to the office, he took the revolver that Sorel had left in the drawer of the desk, and slipped it into his pocket. Then he set off along the road to Dupont's. But this time the whole place was in darkness, so that the buildings loomed up with sudden unexpectedness against the night. The cubicles were in darkness too. Alf went to the door of the end one and tapped.

No answer came, but he thought he heard a stirring inside. He tapped once more. This time a light flickered. A candle was lit. The door was thrown violently open.

Camille stood within, wearing a hooded cloak, and behind her Alf saw

Philippe. There was nothing in the cubicle, which was completely bare. Recoiling in astonishment Alf heard Camille's voice speaking in cold and utterly passionless tones: 'Yes, you were right, Philippe. It's quite true, what you told me, that Monsieur Collet knows the way here, and I am no longer ashamed that I put your story to the test.'

'You are satisfied now, sister?'

'I'm satisfied.' She drew the cloak closer about her. 'Please take me home now, Philippe.'

'*Camille!*' The name broke like a cry from Alf's lips. He was hardly beginning to understand.

'My sister does not wish to speak to you, Monsieur Collet,' interposed Philippe.

Alf heard a sniggering sound behind him. He spun about. Through the dark he saw Egan's face projected, as if upon a screen. In that darkness Alf had the curious optical illusion that Egan was nothing but a face. He seemed cut off at the throat. Camille, at the sight of him, started, and looked fixedly at Philippe.

'I don't quite get this,' said Alf. 'I had a message from Celeste Trudeau asking me to come at once. I understood she needed me.'

Again Egan's snigger rang out, and now Alf understood. He saw the fatuousness of his plea. Every word he spoke only confirmed Camille's opinion of him. She stood, rigid as a statue. She did not deign to answer him. She simply turned away.

Alf looked at the three helplessly. It was so trivial, so fatuous — surely Camille could not believe that he had come to see Celeste as her lover! Not if she cared for him at all, or believed in him. But she was going. Alf did not know what to do.

But Philippe touched his sister on the arm. 'It is understood that Monsieur Collet's services are no longer needed at the mill,' he suggested.

'Monsieur Collet will have the good sense to know where he is required and where he is not,' Camille replied.

They were moving away. Alf's indignation burst the bonds of indecision. He stepped forward and grasped Philippe by the shoulder.

'Monsieur Collet, I do not wish to listen to you,' Philippe exclaimed.

'Maybe not,' answered Alf, 'but you're going to all the same. And you, Mademoiselle Destry,' he added as she looked coldly away, but stopped irresolutely, 'what I've got to say is this. This thing's a lie, and just as dirty a lie as the man who thought of it's a liar. And I guess you know as much about it as that man there. But I'm not saying any more about that part of the business just at present; it doesn't seem to me worthwhile. If your sister likes to believe such a thing as that — all right.

'But that's got nothing to do with the business. I've got your property back for you from the men who stole it, and I'm not going to let you and Mademoiselle Camille be jockeyed out of it by any trumped up business like this. I'm not going to leave the mill — not until you or your sister are ready to take over the charge of it, without any chance of its being taken away again. I'm going to call the men together in the morning and tell them that. They'll follow me.'

He choked down the sickening doubt that accompanied his words. Would the men follow him? 'I'm not going to step out and hand back your mill to that man,' he continued, pointing to the squat figure of Egan, grossly outlined in the darkness.

Philippe glanced at Egan. Alf fancied there was a subtle understanding in that look. 'Ah, yes, Monsieur Collet, you are certainly going,' he said.

Egan sniggered out of the obscurity. 'I guess Collet's goin' to take that back,' he said. 'He's goin' to kiss St. Laurent goodbye tomorrer, and he ain't comin' back. He's a wise guy, but he's bid too high on a pair of two-spots, and — I guess I got the joker.'

'You see, monsieur,' said Philippe, 'there has been a good deal of trouble here, but now it is all settled and we no longer require your services. So you will be satisfied to go.'

But he was glancing shiftily about him as he spoke, as if he were playing for time. Now Alf began to have an undefinable sense that something was behind all this. Again the suspicion of a premeditated attack came over him. Yet Camille's presence seemed to give the lie to that suspicion.

But something was behind it. The tenseness of the atmosphere was near the breaking point. Alf glanced at Camille's white face, at Egan, at Philippe, at Celeste, standing in a strained attitude with clasped hands. He backed against the wall of the shack, holding his revolver ready.

'We'd better understand each other,' he said. 'I told you I'm not going, Monsieur Destry, and I meant that. I'll go when your sister's a free agent and discharges me. Then I'll go — when she's taken over the mill. I'm not going to be fired out by a committee. And when I go, I'll know who's to supersede me.' He pointed to Egan. 'Mademoiselle Destry,' he cried, 'is it your wish that *this man* should take my place?'

Camille made no reply. She was still standing rigid at Philippe's side, her face perfectly immobile, her eyes looking into vacancy. And the long silence that ensued was, Alf knew, at once the springing of

279

the trap and the culmination of every-thing.

The springing of the trap which had not yet been sprung! Alf knew it before it closed, before Egan had spoken a word. Egan stepped forward, a look of wicked triumph on his face.

'I guess it's time to give the knockout,' he said to Philippe. He turned to Alf. 'I've been wise to you fer a good while now,' he said, 'you lyin' jailbird. I ain't perfect. I've had my ups and downs meself, and when I started in to make a new job of things mebbe I changed my name, meanin' to run straight under a new one. Mebbe my name ain't Smith at all, but somethin' else.

'Let's suppose it was Egan. Yeah, I guess it must have been Egan, because that's the name you called me by without knowin' it, that day we had that talk together, when you was tryin' to git me to go in with you and burglarise Sorel's safe. Soon as I saw you here, I kinder thought I'd lamped you before. Thought at first you was a dick, mebbe, and had followed me up here. But I couldn't place you, and

280

I was beginnin' to think I'd made a mistake until that time you called me Egan. Then I spotted you fer the murderin' jailbird that you are. Mademoiselle Destry!' Egan shouted, pointing a long finger at Alf, '*that's the man who killed your father!*'

Camille uttered a cry and ran forward to where Alf was standing. 'Is that true?' she demanded fiercely. 'Is it true? If it's a lie, *tell him so!*'

'It ain't no lie,' said Egan. 'That's the bird who killed your father. Battered him to death in Fall City something over four years ago. Beat him to death in the gutter fer his money, and got a life term fer it, and broke away from the pen and come up here to blackmail you and me and Sorel. And I kept his secret fer him. Goin' to stay, is he? Well, I guess he ain't. He's got somethin' more comin' to him yet. Look at him again and ask him again if he's your father's murderer or no!'

Under the blow of Egan's unexpected denunciation Alf had the persistent impression that it was all a dream. He heard Egan's words as if they were

281

addressed to another, and looking with a strange, observant detachment at Philippe, he saw now that he had been in the plot from the beginning.

And again Camille was crying: 'Is it true? Is it true? Why don't you answer me?'

'It's true,' answered Alf quietly, 'so far as the part goes about me having got a life term on the charge of killing your father and breaking away. But it's not true I killed him. And I guess Egan knows who did. And it's not true I came up here with the idea of getting blackmail, neither. I came up here because I'd had word that this man Egan was here, to force the truth out of his lying throat — and *I'm going to now!*' And in another instant he would have hurled himself upon him.

Egan put up his hand. 'Nix on that,' he answered, and whistled.

And in that instant the darkness was alive with shouts and scurrying figures. Now Dupont's groggery suddenly blazed with lights as it gave up its ambuscade. They were all about him; Alf, struggling to reach Egan, was tossed away, beaten, battered, and flung, half-stunned, to the ground. For a few minutes he lost consciousness.

A minute later he opened his eyes, to find himself lying upon Dupont's little porch, in the centre of a group of men. Camille's white face was visible among them. One of Alf's captors held a pistol to his head. Alf tapped his elbow against the pocket which had held the revolver; it was empty. He sat up. He staggered to his feet, and leaned against a post, his captors ringing him.

Then out of the group there stepped a man, the sight of whom sent a chill of horror through Alf's heart. Dizzy from the blows he had received, Alf stared at him through the swirling mists, seeing only him. He knew that face well enough; it had been graven indelibly upon his memory; he had dreamed of it in nightmares, and he had prayed that he might never see it again. It was the face of the deputy-warden of the penitentiary.

'You identify him?' inquired the man with the pistol, without turning his head.

'Well, I guess so,' answered Johnson. 'I

ought to, if anybody did. Well, well, four twenny-four, guess you treated yourself to a good run for your money, didn't you! Sure I identify him, Sheriff. That's the man mentioned in the extradition papers, and if you'll bring him along to Montreal we'll have things fixed up in next to no time.'

Camille's voice rang out: 'So now we know the truth! I'm glad, Philippe! Take me home — don't speak to me, but take me home!'

And, sobbing, she collapsed and clung limply to her brother, her arms about his neck. And there was a sub-note in Camille's voice that aroused Alf to frenzy. It was a note of vindictive joy, of triumph. And in the bitterness of that moment Alf became once more the wild beast that had escaped from the penitentiary.

The world went black. For just an instant he stood dead; then he hurled himself upon the man with the pistol. It roared; but, taken off his guard, the man fired crookedly. The heavy bullet whizzed past Alf's ear and thudded into the wall of Dupont's groggery. The next moment, Alf had wrenched the pistol from the man's grasp.

All fell back in confusion before the menace. Before they had recovered themselves Alf had burst through them and gained the forest.

Then they were after him like a pack of wolves in chase. Alf had turned toward the river, and this gave them the advantage, for he found himself on continually descending ground, and they were above him, surrounding him on three sides, cutting off his escape completely. They were pressing on him. They were gaining. A pistol cracked. Alf saw them emerge out of the pines at the edge of the open space about the rollways. The rollways were immediately in front of him. There was no other choice; death or the pen.

Alf hardly hesitated upon the brink. As his pursuers, with yells of triumph, closed on him, he leaped and went plunging through the darkness toward the icy torrent below.

24

'Don't speak to me — take me home!'

Shuddering, Camille put her arm through Philippe's and accompanied him down the trail. The news of Alf's leap, brought back by some of the party, seemed to have severed the thinking part of her from the emotional part; numbed, she was conscious only of a great horror.

The sheriff and his deputies were beating the gorge, but there seemed hardly a possibility that Alf's body would be found. The icy stream would toss it among the rocks and bear it down to the dam, where it would be found next day.

Only once Camille spoke on the way homeward: 'I should have thought better of you, Philippe, if you had not secretly arranged that dénouement with Monsieur Smith.'

Philippe made no reply. When one is secure in victory one can afford to let others cavil about the means. With a demonstration of affection he drew his sister's arm through his own.

At the door of their cabin Camille spoke again. 'I'm glad,' she said fiercely. 'Philippe, you will never mention his name again. We must forget all that has happened — everything, since he came here.'

Philippe led her inside the cabin. He lit a lamp and carried it to her room. She went in. She flung herself down on the bed, and lay there with compressed lips and eyes that stared out without seeing anything. So all was over. He was dead, and her love was dead. The little dream was shattered, but then that had all been inevitable from the beginning. She exulted in the sacrifice of her love. With a fury of revulsion she hated even the memory of the dead man.

But what now?

Lying there, so tense was the conflict of feelings with in her that she passed into a kind of trance-like condition, seeing and hearing nothing, her entire faculties concentrated upon that inner struggle. It might have been minutes or hours before she came back to herself, conscious of the low muttering of voices in the cabin.

She sat up on the bed and listened. The voices came from the dining-room, and they went on and on. At first Camille thought Philippe had been drinking and was talking to himself; then she discovered that there were two speakers. She rose up and went softly to the door. That of the living-room was not quite closed. She stood outside for a moment or two, and then, disdaining to play the listener in her own home, went in.

Philippe and Egan were sitting close together, crouched up in chairs. On a table between them were a bottle of whisky and two tumblers. The bottle was nearly empty, but neither man displayed the least sign of being under the influence of the hooch.

At Camille's sudden entrance, Philippe jumped nervously to his feet. Egan turned round and rose slowly, half-crouching. There was a dreadful gloating leer upon his face. The quivering lamp flame sent the shadow of the hump on his deformed shoulder dancing up and down upon the wall behind him.

And as Camille stood there in silence, watching them, she felt that this was the crucial moment, and she waited for it, as a man waits for his fate, a little curious as to the outcome, but no longer capable of any emotion. And through an eternity Egan was slowly assuming an upright posture, and with it, it seemed, the other aspects of a human being.

'Well, he's done fer,' he said.

'What are you doing here with my brother?' asked Camille with quiet contempt.

'Hey?' jeered Egan, fixing her with a look of amused satisfaction. 'Why, I jest come here to talk things over, mademoiselle. I done a good job, and I want my pay fer it.'

'Pay? Talk to your tools, then. I didn't employ you.'

'And it'll be *you*!' said Egan succinctly, with a look that suddenly grew wolfish.

Camille's clear laugh rang through the little room. 'You've had your answer long ago, Mr. Smith,' she returned.

Egan's face became suffused with

blood. He strode toward Camille and grasped her by the wrists, thrusting his face into hers. 'By God, there ain't goin' to be no double-crossin' in this deal!' he shouted. 'I done my part fer you, and you're goin' to do yours!'

Camille, without resisting or raising her voice, turned to her brother. 'Philippe, are you going to protect me?' she asked quietly.

Philippe suddenly bounded into action. 'Take your hands off my sister, Monsieur Smith!' he shouted excitedly. 'Yes, it *is* my business to protect her. *I* am the seigneur here!'

Egan, without releasing Camille, turned his sneering face toward him. 'Say, Philippe, you come off that high horse of yours before I pull you off!' he answered. 'Take another drink and then I'll talk some more sense to you. You ain't had your bottle tonight, and you don't git things straight. You think I'm goin' to be bluffed now, after I got rid of Collet fer you — ?'

But with a shrill cry, Philippe suddenly leaped at him and struck him in the face.

Egan dropped Camille's wrists and turned on him with a snarl. So savage was Philippe's fury that for a few moments he was Egan's master. He drove him back across the room, landing blow after blow upon him.

Then Egan got his fists into action and sent Philippe staggering back. Then, with cool brutality, he delivered a well-aimed blow that sent him sprawling to the floor, where he lay blinking, half-dazed.

Camille sprang at Egan. He turned on her, pinioning her arms to her sides, and grinning at the futility of her struggles. He forced her backward, held her against the wall, and again thrust his face into hers.

'Now, sister, you and me are goin' to understand each other,' he said. 'The days when you had me on a string and played fast and loose is past. I'm the boss now. Get that?'

Her terror of the man was mightier than her anger. Instinctively she divined that lust and cruelty were combined in him, that any resistance on her part would only endanger her. Shuddering, she went suddenly limp in his clutch.

Egan released her and stood surveying her with a leer.

'That's better, sister,' he mocked. 'I guess you're gettin' wise to the situation at last. When I got a balky horse or a tricky woman to deal with, I deal straight and to the point. Them soft-soap days are past. I don't blame you fer thinkin' you kin work the old gags again, but you can't. I done my part, and you're goin' to pay. And tomorrow you and me are goin' to come to a straight showdown. Git that? Now git back into your room, and don't come buttin' into men's conversation again!'

He opened the door and took her by the arm. But in the passage she twisted herself away from him, ran into her room, slammed the door, and with shaking fingers shot back the bolt that she had put on after the night when Egan had last come to the cabin. Trembling, she crouched upon the other side. If Egan tried to force the flimsy board planks they would not offer much resistance. She glanced desperately about her. Through the little window she saw the soft flakes of the falling snow, black against the lamplight. If Egan attacked the door she would climb through that and run out into the snow.

But he went back into the living-room, and after a few moments her terror began to subside. The glance at the window had brought back the old train of thought. She must leave at once, with Philippe, if she could get him to come, but if not, then without him. She must never see Egan again.

In the next room the muttering had been resumed. With her ear against the thin pine-plank partition Camille tried to listen. But not a word was audible, and she could hear only the same monotonous sounds. Turning away, she began hastily to gather a few things together into a pack. When Egan was gone she would get bread from the kitchen, her snow-shoes . . .

It seemed an eternity before she heard Egan stumping out of the room along the little hall. She listened in breathless suspense. The slam of the front door, which made the cabin vibrate, set her heart to hammering fiercely.

She went into the living-room. Philippe's face was the colour of a corpse. There was the beginning of a dark bruise across his forehead, where Egan had struck him. He was sitting huddled up in his chair, the bottle now empty, lying on the table on its side, his own glass still partly full of the liquor. But, dreadful as his face was, there was a more dreadful look in his eyes. Camille ran to his side. She kneeled down and put her arms about him. She leaned her cheek against his own, and they rested there silently for a minute or two. When at last Philippe spoke she hardly knew the voice for her brother's: 'Camille, do you remember what you were saying to me about leaving everything and going away somewhere where we could be together?'

Her heart leaped at the words. 'Philippe, I have been thinking that. I cannot stay here any longer. All these years . . . it must come to an end.'

'Yes, it must come to an end,' he said drearily.

'Philippe, I am going to say something

to you now that I have never said before. He has you in his power. It is because of that money you took from the safe when our father had gone down over the border to sell the lands. I have known it for a long time. That is where the missing money went to. He had borrowed it from Sorel. That is why I have never dared to demand our rights. The time has come to speak now. Isn't that it?'

He turned his face away and nodded.

'I could not tell him — that dead man. I would never have let it be known. Far better to have lost everything. But Smith knew — that is why he got you into his power. That is why you — you acted as you would never have done otherwise, isn't it?'

Again he nodded, but he did not attempt to meet her eyes. And she went on with her story eagerly: 'You were in Montreal at the time, you remember. You knew the combination. You came back secretly. I always suspected that. And Smith threatens your arrest, you, the seigneur. It could not be endured.

'Yes, that is it, Camille,' responded

295

Philippe, as if he leaped eagerly at her words. 'That is why I — I spoke about going away just now. I could not bear to see you married to him — the swine — it is not to be thought of. I should be disgraced forever. For of course the time will come when we shall be in a far different position, and then what would people say of me, if it were known my sister was the wife of a common fellow like that man Smith?'

For a moment Camille gazed at him despairingly; she could see that the liquor had actually affected his mind. There was always the erratic touch to everything he said, there were hints of the delusion of grandeur in his harping on the future. But she only held him the more closely and said nothing.

'When shall we start, Camille?'

'Tonight — or at dawn. It is as good as any other time.'

'How much money have you?'

'There is little more than forty dollars left, Philippe.'

'If I should go to Smith and tell him some story I could get money from him

— a hundred dollars, perhaps — '

'No, no, it is impossible. Oh, don't you see, Philippe? How could we get money from him like that?'

'No, no, you are quite right,' he answered. 'It would not be in accordance with my position. But where do we go and how far will forty dollars take us?'

'I have been thinking — do you remember our Aunt Jacqueline in Notre Dame des Fontaines? She was the only one of our relatives who wrote to us after our troubles. She would take us in for a while. Then we could go to work, you to the camps, I to sew. We would do anything to earn a living, and we would be happy, and gradually forget the past.'

'But forty dollars would no more than take us to Montreal, Camille, if so far, and Notre Dame des Fontaines is a long way from there. Now I have been thinking. Three days' journey up the river is the camp of the Rochambeau company. I know their foreman, Monsieur Grondet. I met him at Dupont's one Saturday night; he had come down by boat to bring back two of his men, who were drinking there. You have always despised me, Camille, but I have kept my eyes open. I was not working in the dark when I went to Dupont's. Well, Monsieur Grondet has need of a clerk in the company's store, and he will give me the position. And there is a nice little cottage goes with it, where we should be comfortable. And it is three days's journey away. You need have no fear of Smith. If he dares to follow us there I will protect you from him.

'Let us go there, and when we have saved up a little money at the end of the winter, then we can go to Notre Dame des Fontaines. Come, Camille, let us start for the Rochambeau place at dawn. There is a good road all the way, and the first night we can sleep in the old camp that was built there some years ago. There will only be one night in the open, and it is not very cold. I will carry blankets for both of us . . . '

He said it all like a parrot, as if it had been in his mind so long that he had it by rote. But Camille was conscious only of an intense happiness.

'I will go there or anywhere with you,

Philippe,' she answered simply. 'Anywhere so long as we leave St. Laurent forever and never see it, or any of the people here, again.'

25

A dozen times that night, Camille stole to the door of her brother's room, listening to his breathing. He slept — how could he sleep? She felt as if she would never sleep again. She felt divorced from all physical needs and sensations. She was nothing but will, she would be nothing more until St. Laurent was far behind them. She finished packing methodically, she prepared food, forgetting nothing. Then she waited for the dawn.

It came at last in a blaze of red horizon clouds. She closed the two packs, took down their snowshoes, and called Philippe.

At the touch of his sister's hand upon his shoulder, he leaped up in bed in panic, uttering a low cry. He stared at her for some moments before he remembered.

'It is time to start, Philippe.'

'Yes — yes,' he mumbled, sitting up in

the bed and looking at her strangely.

'You remember, Philippe. You have not changed your decision?'

He dropped his eyes, as if in confusion. 'I am willing,' he muttered. 'Only — I was thinking — is there no other way? It is hard to leave St. Laurent — '

Camille always remembered *that* thereafter, whenever she felt bitterest. Philippe had asked her to stay. But she had not the key to his mind. 'Philippe, last night it was all arranged. You remember what was said?'

'Yes, yes, certainly I remember,' he stammered. 'Yes, we will start immediately, Camille. It will be a long day's tramp to the huts, and we must arrive before sundown.'

They set off after a hurried breakfast, on their snowshoes. The snow had ceased to fall, the sun shone in an unclouded sky, and it was intensely cold, one of those sudden onsets of winter that occur in November and almost rival the fierceness of the January spells. The snow was like cinders underfoot. At the head of the trail Camille turned; she was bidding farewell to the Colony forever. It looked so peaceful, the little valley, with the clusters of cabins dotted about it. What would happen to the *habitants* there? She had no longer the heart to care. She was fleeing to save Philippe from a felon's cell, and she repeated to herself insistently that he was a thief; she seemed to glory in it for some cause which she would not admit into her mind. A thief! He had stolen and squandered Sorel's money, and Sorel, for some purpose of his own, probably through fear, had said nothing. And so insistent was her desire to fix this in her mind that she turned suddenly upon Philippe.

'It is because you stole that money that Smith holds you in his power, Philippe!' she said.

'*Ma foi*, yes.' He shrugged his shoulders. 'I had a debt of honour . . . women do not understand such things.'

No,' answered Camille, 'we do not understand.'

The trail which they had taken struck the track along the river about a mile above Dupont's. The gorge was even higher, and the river bed more rocky for fully twenty miles above, until the abandoned lumber camp was reached, from which the upper courses of the stream were a smooth and shallow channel. A number of confluents met at a point just below this camp, where they united, tumbling over a rocky ledge to form the main body of water, and this site had been selected by the Rochambeau company as the head of the navigable portion of the river, and the uppermost point from which logs could be floated downstream.

The river, always swift, had now been converted into a swirling torrent by the snows of the past week, and already large cakes of ice went tossing down on its black waters, while thin ice sheathed the banks and extended out toward the middle stream. Camille looked down and shuddered as she thought of what Alf's fate must have been. And she stilled the wild pang in her heart by remembering his treachery, and his deception of her.

What had he been? A score of times she had asked herself that question. A spy, most likely, sent up to investigate the circumstances of her father's death . . . She drove all thoughts of the dead man from her, and they went on and on through the white landscape. With every mile her heart rose. She could learn to forget the past, away from St. Laurent.

They ate at noon, rested a brief while, and resumed their journey. But toward the middle of the afternoon Philippe began to flag. At last he came to a stop. Looking at him, Camille saw that his face was drawn and white.

He unstrapped his pack and began searching in it. He stared at her in dismay. '*Diable!*' he muttered. 'There was a half-bottle that I was keeping; I have forgotten it.'

'Philippe,' she said earnestly, 'there must be no more drinking. Now that we have left St. Laurent you must give it up forever. It will not be impossible, will it, Philippe?'

'No, no, it is easy. I can always stop drinking when I want to. But, you see, one has to break off gradually, and after last night . . . my nerves . . . '

He put his pack together with shaking fingers, and they went on. At last he stopped again. '*Maudit*, I cannot bear it!' he muttered, clutching at his throat. 'I must go back for a bottle, Camille — just as far as Dupont's. Smith will not be there. Dupont will let me have a bottle, and I shall say nothing about ourselves.'

'No, no, you must come on, Philippe. It would be madness to turn back now. Once this attack is over you will not feel the need of liquor.'

She took him by the arm, and he went with her, grumbling. The sun was dipping toward the horizon. Half a dozen times he stopped to argue the matter, but always she persuaded him to go on.

'Listen,' she said the last time he stopped, 'there are the falls; do you not hear them roaring? The huts will be in sight in a few minutes.' Again he went on with her, leaning heavily upon her for support. His face was twitching, and it was evident that the nervous tension had become acute. Topping a rise, they saw the huts of the abandoned camp in the distance. Camille pointed them out to

305

him. He looked at her apathetically, shrugged his shoulders, and went on.

The last quarter of a mile was measured almost by feet. Even more than the nervous tension was the irresolution that Philippe showed. He stopped every few yards, hesitant, and it was always Camille who seized his arm tighter and drew him on. At length, however, just as the sun dipped on the horizon, they reached the camp. It consisted of a number of bunkhouses, a cookhouse, and a store and office, all rotting, leaking, and falling to pieces under the weather. Camille chose the office as the driest of them all. In it there was a bare bunk. She made Philippe lie down and put his pack under his head.

'You will not stir until I return?' she asked. 'I am going for water; then I shall light a fire in the cookhouse stove. You will feel better after you have had some coffee.'

He promised her, and Camille got a pail that was in a corner of the cookhouse, and went down to the water. The roaring floods were pouring over the falls in a miniature cataract. Clambering down the gorge, she broke the ice at the edge of the stream and drew water. She stood for a few moments, absorbed in the melancholy wildness of the scene, the waste of the turbulent eddies over the rocky ledge, the gloom of the snow-laden trees that overhung the river. Then she re-ascended the slope and made her way back.

Glancing in at the office, she saw Philippe lying where she had left him, apparently asleep. She prepared strong coffee in the cookhouse, with pancakes, and brought them to him. For a while she stood beside him, hesitating to wake him. She looked at him with a little pity, remembering the olden days when they had been children together. How sordidly his theft had reacted on him, what a bitter punishment, that slow degradation of a man.

Suddenly Philippe opened his eyes. He leaped up in the bunk, clutching his throat. 'I'm burning!' he cried. 'I must have liquor   a little liquor to taper off on!'

Camille handed him the coffee. 'Drink this and you will feel better,' she said.

He swallowed a few mouthfuls and pushed the tin pannikin away, upsetting it. He caught at Camille's hand. 'You must go back to Dupont's for me!' he cried. 'I'm *dying*, I tell you. Only one bottle, a little each day, until I am free from the desire. You don't want me to die?' And he began pleading, the tears starting to his eyes.

'Philippe, by the time I got back you would already have gone through the worst,' said Camille. 'You must fight it out. It's the only way. I'll make you some more coffee, *stronger coffee*.'

He would not listen. His pleadings changed to taunts, threats. He reviled her. She had never heard such words as now came from his lips. 'Eh, you have always thought yourself the seigneur and not me!' he jeered. 'But I haven't been working in the dark. I saw where our interests lay. You have been nothing but my tool, playing my game — my tool, do you hear? God, I must have some whisky! I'm going back!'

He leaped to his feet and started toward the door, but Camille resolutely barred the way. She knew he would not dare to lay his hands upon her, and he did not, but stood regarding her with envenomed malice.

'Eh, Camille, you have been a play-thing, that's all!' he jeered at her. 'You believed that Collet went to Dupont to see that woman Celeste, eh, sister? Well, she was Smith's woman until he grew tired of her, and she was too infatuated with Smith even to think of another man, even of young Collet. She followed Smith to St. Laurent from Montreal. Everybody knew it except you, who think you know everything. That poor fool, Collet, was trying to help her. It was a trick message that brought him there last night. You have been made a fine fool of! You are so simple, sister!'

Camille, white to the lips, regarded Philippe silently. She felt that this did not matter, that nothing mattered; she knew in her heart she had never believed that Alf was Celeste's lover. She knew that it was only an excuse she had leaped at.

'Let me pass! I tell you I am going back for a bottle!'

'You are not going to pass, Philippe. You had better lie down and let me make you some more coffee; you will soon feel better.'

Philippe stood glaring at her. 'I'll tell you something more!' he babbled. He was working himself into an artificial rage, she saw that, but could not divine the cause. 'I'll tell you something more. You think I stole our father's money from the safe. You are so easy to fool. Well, I did not. There was no money. Now I am going to tell you — '

'*Philippe!*' Her voice was a startled cry. 'Nothing of that. It is all past. Not a word of that, I tell you!'

He leered at her distress. Then suddenly he clutched his head in an acute paroxysm, and fell across the bunk. He staggered to his feet again, moaning.

'Let me pass, sister, and I will tell you nothing. Let me pass, then.'

'You cannot go to Dupont's. It is madness. You would fall in the snow.'

'I'm going back, I say! The devil

himself shan't stop me.'

'No, you are not going back, Philippe, and you are not going to strike me.'

His upraised fist fell. A twisted look came on his face. Suddenly his demeanour changed.

'Eh, little sister,' he said in a wheedling tone, 'it shall be as you say. You have been a good little sister to me, and I have been a fool.'

She was becoming frightened. Philippe's craft, always transparent, terrified her as his violence never did.

'Sister, there is no air in here, and I am choking. I want to go down to the river. Listen, little sister. You shall hold my arm and walk along the gorge with me. You know that I could easily force my way past you out of this room, only I would never lay my hands upon you; well, then, it will be the same outside. You shall hold me all the time. I see that it would be folly to start back to Dupont's. The cold air may cure me. I am choking.'

He tore at his throat in another paroxysm. Camille hesitated, then drew his arm through hers and led him from the hut down toward the river. The stars shone brightly in the sky. The night air was bitter cold. The roaring of the torrent filled their ears.

Camille expected Philippe to make a dash for liberty, but he did not; he accompanied her, staggering in his walk toward the gorge. They stopped upon the brink.

'Let us go down to the water's edge, sister,' he wheedled.

She looked at him, trying to pierce the fog of his intentions. But there was no road back to Dupont's beside the water below the gorge. They began the descent, picking their way among the rocks until they reached the icy edge of the torrent. A little strip of sandy shore led to a projecting boulder, the farther side veiled with dense evergreens. Philippe started aimlessly toward it. Suddenly, within a few paces of it, Camille stopped.

'There is a boat anchored there!' she exclaimed.

The next instant, three men leaped from behind the boulder and came at a run toward them. As one recognises a face in a disordered nightmare, Camille recognised Egan and the two Papineaus.

Philippe dragged himself free and swung her toward Egan.

'*There's* your blood-money, *you devil*!' he roared; and, howling like a demented man, he began scrambling up the precipice.

26

Alf owed his life to something whose existence he had forgotten — the dump of sand beneath the rollways placed there for the construction of the upper dam. The chance of his leap hurled him upon this instead of into the torrent. The light snow had protected it from freezing, and he descended upon a yielding bed.

For a minute or two he lay there dazed, at the water's edge, hearing the shouts above him die away. Then, as the clear memory of the events of that night came back to him, there accompanied them the determination not to be taken.

For him St. Laurent was ended, and Camille's defection had renewed all his old bitterness of spirit, which had thawed insensibly with the dawning of his love. St. Laurent was ended, and, for the present, at any rate, his hope of establishing his innocence.

And in his bitterness, he saw that in

spite of all his resolutions he had again fallen into his fatal error of weakness. If he had played his own hand steadily, instead of espousing Camille's cause, only to be betrayed, he might at least have saved himself from leaving St. Laurent in this ignominious fashion.

The sheriff and his deputies had made no examination of the gorge. Little could have been done in the darkness, and without a doubt they were satisfied that Alf was dead. This gave him until morning, and by morning he meant to be far away. He knew roughly the lie of the country. By striking upstream for a considerable distance, he could reach an old tote-road of one of the lumber companies, which would eventually take him southward by a very roundabout route. For food he must rely on chance, or on striking a lumber camp. And Alf knew all about the food proposition, and just how long one could starve.

Pulling himself together, he began to chafe his bruised limbs, which were already beginning to stiffen. Then he started to pick his way along the bottom of the gorge. He decided that it would be wiser to cover a few miles in this fashion before ascending to the trail, in case he met anyone there who would give the alarm.

He began to stumble along the narrow edge of the gorge, between the precipice and the ice edging of the torrent. Progress was slow, and it was not long before he discovered that he was hurt worse than he had thought. There was an increasing pain in his side, as if a rib were broken, and an unlucky fall over a rock wrenched his knee, and made progress still more difficult. The cold, too, had become biting. Time spun out confusedly, and Alf had no idea how much distance he had covered when at length he decided that he could proceed no farther except along the trail.

He was about to begin the ascent of the precipice when suddenly the faint flicker of a light around the bend of the gorge attracted his attention.

Creeping nearer, he saw that it was the light of a campfire. But why anyone should have selected the bed of the stream for a camping place he could not imagine.

When he came within a score of yards of it, he saw that the fire was burning inside a small cave in the flank of the gorge, throwing its reflection on the rocks around it. Feeling reassured, he approached, and, peering into the cave, he saw a man and a woman seated beside some blazing birch logs.

They glanced up and saw him. They sprang to their feet in alarm. The woman shrank back; the man came toward him in a threatening manner. The next moment, Alf recognised Charles Bartel. And the woman with him was Celeste Trudeau.

Charles stopped short and stared at him. His jaw dropped. 'It is you, Monsieur Collet?' he stammered.

Alf staggered in and dropped beside the fire from weariness. Celeste ran toward him. 'Why, your head is bleeding, monsieur!' she exclaimed in concern. 'You have had an accident?'

'Yes, a sort of accident,' answered Alf grimly

Celeste began to make a bandage.

Charles Bartel drew near, and, seeing that he was looking at him suspiciously, Alf said: 'There's nothing to be afraid of from me. I'm making my getaway from St. Laurent. The sheriff came for me. I'm wanted for something that I'm supposed to have done in America. I jumped over the rollways and landed on a pile of sand.'

'*Ma foi!*' exclaimed Charles, grasping him by the hand. 'And me, too, monsieur. You see, Celeste heard that the sheriff was expected, and, being fearful for me, she managed to warn me. *Tiens*, so it was for *you* he came! But no matter. We are travelling together.

'We go north to St. Paul, where there is a missionary station for the Indians, and there we are married. And then it is the new life for us with the traps — you understand, monsieur?'

Alf grasped Charles's hand. 'I wish you luck, both of you,' he said.

'Monsieur Collet must stay with us, and perhaps we shall travel together — is it not so, monsieur?' inquired Celeste. 'Charles, get the coffee.' And as he went to his pack, she turned to Alf hurriedly.

318

'Monsieur Collet,' she said in an earnest whisper, 'there is one thing I implore of you. You will not tell him that Monsieur Smith is at St. Laurent. I have made him think that he has long since departed. If he knew, he would go back and kill him. And he has forgiven me and we are going to be happy.'

Alf promised her, and next moment Charles came back with the coffee. The hot draught made Alf feel better. Then they made their plans. It was arranged that the three should travel in company as far as the road by which Alf meant to make his way toward Montreal. Later, when Celeste had withdrawn to sleep upon a bed of pine branches at the back of the cave, leaving the two men sitting over the fire together, Charles told Alf his story.

'Monsieur, I am a happy man, and I think, on the whole, a lucky one,' he said. 'That poor woman was lied to and deceived by this dog Smith, who appears to know me, though I cannot recall him. And she understands that all the past is buried. And for me, too. Monsieur, when

I went to America, to earn the money for our marriage, I looked forward to an early return and a happy life with her. But times were bad, and there was a man named Egan — that was four years ago — who offered me money to act as look-out for a gang that was robbing the warehouses. I took it, monsieur, because I was hungry — and that placed me in Egan's power.

'Then he came to me one day and demanded that I should commit a far worse crime, or he would betray me to the police. In brief, monsieur, it was to act as lookout for a murderer. There was an old rich man who would be passing a certain street, and he was to be robbed and killed. I was to act as look-out for the man Murphy, who was to kill him — '

'Murphy!' shouted Alf.

Bartel looked at him in surprise. 'Why — but you do not know him, Monsieur Collet?' he asked.

'No — never mind; go on,' said Alf, controlling himself with difficulty.

'You will hardly understand, Monsieur Collet, how a man comes to sink lower and lower until the things that he would once have looked upon with horror become natural for him. Unless I agreed Egan threatened to have me arrested. And the police were looking for the warehouse thieves. In brief, I consented to meet Murphy at a certain hour, and to watch, while he killed the old man.

'I was there at the time. But Murphy had not arrived when I saw the old man coming. He came so slow, and I was afraid. It was a dark night and a little foggy. I wanted to go to him and warn him. Then I hoped he would pass the spot before Murphy arrived. But I looked back, and there was Murphy coming, and I saw the iron bar in his hand. In those few moments I spent an eternity in hell, monsieur.

'There was I, at the corner of the street, from which I could watch and give the warning, and the old man coming one way, and Murphy coming toward him from the other, and in a few moments the two would meet. And then, monsieur, something happened which saved me from the crime of murder.

'Suddenly out of the fog appeared a third man. He, too, must have been following the old man, for he approached him suddenly. There was a swift exchange of angry words; I saw the third man lift his arm and strike. The old man dropped. And then I ran.

'And so, monsieur, *le bon Dieu* saved my soul from the stain of murder. But after that Egan would not let me go. He said that it was known at my home, across the lake, that the police wanted me. And ever since I have been afraid to return, though once I came up as far as St. Joseph — why, it was you sent me back, monsieur!' he cried in sudden recognition.

'Do you know who the old man was?' asked Alf.

'Ah, no, monsieur, how should I?'

Alf reflected that in all probability Bartel did not even know of Destry's death. 'And the man who killed him — was he a young man, or an old one?'

'How should I know, monsieur? It was only for a few moments that I saw his face in the fog. But I should know it to the end

322

of my life if I ever saw it again.'

Alf lay awake that night in the same bitterness of spirit. He had profited nothing from Bartel's story. It was easy to piece the fragments together, and to see that Egan had been using Bartel as he had used him, covering his own slimy trail with an infinitude of precautions. Then, doubtless, Sorel had intervened and killed Destry.

The story had availed Alf nothing. And, putting aside the momentary hope that had been born in him, Alf composed himself to sleep.

He awoke sore and stiff, but an examination convinced him that the rib was not broken, and his wrenched knee was paining him little. In this district there was little likelihood of their meeting anyone, and the three took to the trail that morning and made substantial progress by noon. Celeste leaned upon Charles's arm as they walked, and her face seemed transfigured with happiness.

They halted for an hour at noon and went on again. Toward sundown, the roar of the torrent grew louder; they were approaching the waterfalls. The sun was just dipping into the horizon when another sound came to their ears and halted them. It died away, and then burst out again, louder, and now unmistakable. It was the chugging of a motorboat, coming upstream.

They looked at one another in dismay. Charles took Alf by the arm. 'Monsieur,' he stammered, 'it must be — '

'The sheriff, yes.'

They looked hurriedly about them. It was still light, and the barren stretch of burned over country that they were traversing afforded them no refuge. The only safe hiding-place was among the trees and rocks at the edge of the gorge. They began to clamber down, crouching low in the underbrush as the sound of the boat's engine grew louder.

'Here is a place,' said Celeste, pointing to a depression in the wall of the gorge, concealed by some large boulders.

They scrambled over them and crouched in the entrance. Shielded by the rocks and the low-growing spruce scrub that had found lodgment in the crevices, they were safe from discovery, while it would be possible to view the occupants of the boat as it went by.

'They must stop here; they cannot go up the cataract,' whispered Bartel as the boat shot round the point.

The next instant, they saw that the boat was putting ashore on their side of the river. But it was now growing dark in the gorge, and the rocks immediately in front of them concealed the forms of the three men, who landed immediately opposite the cave and made preparations for camping.

Brush was gathered, and soon the flame of a fire shot up. The voices of the three came to the fugitives, at first as a confused sound, then louder, as the hooch began to circulate.

'I think,' said Charles Bartel with conviction, 'that that is not the sheriff and his men.'

And quietly he began to worm his way among the boulders until he was clear of the cave. Lying flat in the underbrush, he parted it and peered through it. Then he came back in the same way. 'It is not the sheriff, it is Egan and two *Canayens*, one of whom looks like my friend Alphonse,' he said. '*Tiens*, it *is* Egan. I am not mistaken. And now — '

Suddenly his face was lit up with furious passion. He caught Celeste by the wrist. 'Now — *that name!*' he hissed. '*Egan!* Egan here! That Smith! *Diable*, am I a fool or a child?'

He whipped out a revolver from his coat pocket. 'Eh, I was right!' he cried.

Celeste clung to him. 'Charles, you are not going to kill him?' she pleaded. 'Ah, Charles, be quiet! They will hear us . . . and Monsieur Collet here . . . '

'*This* is your Monsieur Smith, *this* Egan!' cried Bartel still more loudly. 'He dies *now — I have sworn it!*'

With a sudden wrench of her wrist Celeste got the weapon from him, and, fully of his own strength, and overtopping him by an inch or two, she fought back on equal terms. He made no attempt to harm her, but he struggled desperately to break her clasp on the revolver.

Upon the point of intervention, Alf suddenly saw a man and woman approaching them along the narrow strip of the shore. Looking out through the obscurity, he fancied she was Camille.

The next moment he saw Egan and the two Papineaus rush toward her, and heard Philippe's wild cry. He heard Camille scream as she recognised the trap she had fallen into.

Then he was rushing to her aid, and everything but Camille was forgotten.

27

Egan seized her in his arms. 'I've got you, Camille!' he cried exultantly. 'I swore I'd have you. Mebbe you'll think different about marryin' me tomorrow!'

But with a desperate effort, Camille succeeded in shaking Egan off. With a loud cry she turned and raced blindly along the shore. Next instant Alf was upon Egan from behind.

With one blow he sent him sprawling among the rocks. As he attempted to follow the fleeing figure Aristide barred the way. He dealt the monster a blow in the stomach which momentarily stopped him, evaded the great arms and followed Camille.

Behind him came Charles Bartel. He had not succeeded in wrenching the revolver out of Celeste's hands, and in his blind fury had snatched up a stone with which he rushed on Egan. Warned by Alphonse's cry, Egan, who was in the act of firing a shot at Alf's retreating figure, turned. His bullet hissed past Bartel's head. Bartel came on. A second bullet caught him in the chest and spun him round like a teetotum. As Bartel staggered under its impact, Aristide, whose slow mind had not yet taken in the situation, came shambling forward with growls of anticipatory vengeance, his huge arms threshing the air.

Then Celeste fired from behind the falling body of Charles, and shot Aristide through the forehead. The great mass reeled, released its hold of Charles; and, staring blindly upward, with a single, unhuman cry, Aristide plunged face downward into the sand.

Celeste kneeled over Charles. The blood was welling up from a wound over his heart. Sobbing, and totally forgetful of Egan's presence, she took his head on her lap, and, tearing strips from her skirt, tried to staunch the blood with them.

Egan, whose mind worked quickly, cast only a single glance at them. He had no time to waste, nor was he anxious to waste it on Charles and Celeste. His single mind eliminated secondary matters. Alphonse was tugging at his shoulder and pointing into the darkness.

Camille was no longer visible, but they could still see Alf following her. They set off in pursuit. But through the darkness came Alf's voice, crying to Camille in warning, and in another moment she came into sight, apparently in the heart of the waterfall.

From the point of land that extended below the huts, where two of the upper confluents came together, a narrow ledge of rock jutted out toward the middle of the stream. On either side this had held up the river, which had frozen into great masses of ice, and in the narrow central space between, the full force of the narrowed torrent poured down in a tremendous cascade. Over this ice-bound ledge toward the torrent Camille was running, her arms extended, her loosened hair blown back, her skirts flying behind her, a Maenad, a terrific figure, crazed by fear, and treading that slippery ledge in safety by the same power that is given to sleepwalkers, when the outward faculties are in abeyance. She did not seem to hear Alf's cries or to recognise him.

Then, as Egan and Alphonse drew near, they saw Alf spring upon the ledge and follow her, slipping from side to side upon that foot-wide hold above the churned up ice on the one side, and the boiling torrent below.

They watched with catching breath as Camille, having reached the edge of the torrent, poised herself there as if to leap. A wild, exultant cry came from her lips. She seemed ethereal, unearthly, a creature of the cataract itself. The spray hung over her like a bridal veil.

She had run straight and surely out over the ice-bound ledge to the edge of the waterfall, but Alf, following her, clung to the rocks, slipped over the ice masses, and once lost his foothold, stumbled, caught at a rock and with difficulty pulled himself to the ledge again. All the while Camille remained standing upon the very verge of the torrent, now lost to view amid the spray, now emerging out of it; and once more that wild cry of hers rang out.

They watched with awe as well as terror — even Alphonse and Egan; they watched Alf approaching her. Now he was nearing her. His outstretched hand caught hers.

Then both figures disappeared from sight in the spray.

A terrible cry burst from Egan's lips. He started running madly towards the ledge. He gained his foothold upon it, advanced a few paces, and peered out.

Then he saw them. They had slipped from the ledge and remained caught in some way among the boulders at the edge of the cataract, clinging in a sort of void caused by the suction of the current, a little hollow chamber over which the spray spread fanwise about them.

Egan stared at them in horror, then he started running wildly back.

'The boat, *the boat*, Alphonse!' he yelled. 'We'll get her now!'

'Monsieur, it is impossible,' Alphonse protested.

'*Damn you!*' snarled Egan, raising his fist and striking him in the face.

Alphonse's hand flew to his knife. But

then, dropping it suddenly, he followed Egan to the motorboat. They pushed off into the stream, and Egan started the engine.

At first the swirl of the current bore them swiftly backward; then the engine proved more powerful, and slowly Egan began to drive the boat upstream toward the ledge, keeping inshore to avoid the cataract. In a few minutes the boat was rocking off the ledge, held practically in equipoise between the force of the torrent and the power of the straining engine.

Egan pulled out the rope and cast the anchor about the rocks. From where he was he could see Alf and Camille plainly, not twenty paces from him, wedged among the rocks, Alf still making futile efforts to regain his foothold.

Edged up against the ledge, the boat began to be slowly drawn toward the cataract by the back suction of the whirlpool. The rope tautened. Egan satisfied himself that the anchor was fast and the rope firm. And held by the rope, the boat began to describe a half-circle toward the place where Alf was with

Camille. Slowly it worked around; nearer it came to the two figures.

And, within sight of the final victory, Egan leaned out of the boat and hurled taunts at Alf.

'*I got you, Collet!*' he shouted, trying to out-roar the torrent. 'I got you where I want you, Collet! And I got her!'

There was something so inexpressibly characteristic of the man in this outburst of vulgarity and rancour in the presence of those mighty forces of Nature, that even Alphonse Papineau, without knowing why, despised him. It was a dwarf Prometheus measuring himself against the heavens, but measuring himself in ignorance instead of in the consciousness of the situation that constitutes heroism. The tragic, the stupendous nature of that battle of mind against the elements passed Egan entirely by. He only saw Camille in his power alive, and his enemy, dead.

'You can stay there in cold storage till hell freezes over, Collet!' he cried, and in the consciousness of triumph all the elemental nature of the man came to the surface. It was the subliminal Egan that now burst the bonds of restraint. He jeered and capered as he stood in the bow of the motorboat, ready to reach out and drag Camille from her position among the rocks as soon as the current had nosed the boat into position.

'You hold on to me behind, Alphonse,' he shouted to his supporter. 'One yank, and I'll git her out of there. Hold on and keep the boat steady!'

And stretching out his hands, in imagination he had already grasped Camille round the waist and lifted her aboard.

Absorbed in this attempt, neither Egan nor Alphonse Papineau perceived a third figure that was advancing along the rocky ledge behind them. Like Camille, this figure advanced in apparent unconsciousness of its danger, but as it advanced it writhed and twisted and gesticulated, and perhaps shouted — but if so its cries were absorbed by the thunder of the waterfall, and did not reach the ears of the two men in the boat.

Now it might have been seen that the

figure held a long knife in one hand, and it advanced brandishing and pointing it; and then suddenly it stopped and watched the boat nosing round into position, and seemed to take in the situation.

Now it gesticulated no longer, but continued on its journey with a deliberate purpose that was reflected in the stealthy, panther-like movements. It crouched as it glided onward along the slippery surface of the ledge. And now it was nearing the boat's stern. Now it had reached it. It stopped, crouching over it. Again the knife appeared in the hand. It flashed. There came a downward stroke.

At the wild, bellowing peal of laughter almost in their ears, Egan and Alphonse started and looked round.

'My God, *he's cut the rope!*' howled Alphonse Papineau.

The boat was moving. Already Egan's hand was receding from Camille's shoulder. Egan took in the situation, and with a howl of fury he whipped out his revolver and fired point blank at the figure on the ledge.

It toppled and fell, and in an instant the current had swept it away. Egan ran to the engine and began fumbling wildly and frantically with it as the boat, which now pointed inward toward the cataract, began to gyrate slowly.

But now it was too late. The power of the engine could not, without the fulcrum of the rope, make headway against the torrent. The motorboat, revolving like a top, was being slowly drawn in toward the heart of the whirlpool at the base of the cataract by the back suction of the current.

Bellowing with fear, Alphonse seized an oar and began backing desperately. But the implement was a mere toy against the force that was pulling them to destruction.

Egan, standing in the bow, fixed his gaze on Camille. Perhaps at the last moment something of understanding did come to him; at least he no longer raved and shouted like the frantic man behind him, but stood with folded arms awaiting the inevitable dénouement.

Faster and faster spun the boat. The

cataract, the ledge, the shores revolved in an accelerating reel. Now white water was all about them, the spume of the torrent and the blinding shroud of the mist.

Beneath them the gulf seemed to open, intensely black, a void like the pit of hell into which they were descending. For a moment or two, still pursuing her gyrating movement, the motorboat hung almost vertically upon the edge of it.

Then with a swoop she was gone, to be flung up instantly by the boiling surges. And, their game being ended, they fell upon her and her living freight and flung her to the rocks, and drew her back and battered her into shreds of timbers, as if the teeth of a giant harrow had passed over her.

28

Only as an uncertain nightmare, which he was never after able to recall clearly, had Alf been conscious of the approach of Egan. When he slipped, dragging down Camille with him, he had managed to grasp a fang of rock protruding at the edge of the waterfall, and, by a mighty effort, to lower them both to a larger rock under the outward arc of the white sheet of water.

Drenched by the fine spray, they had nevertheless found lodgment there, in an empty space, almost a vacuum, so strong was the outward suction of the air. The white fall descended in front of them like a curtain, shutting out all sight; underneath the vortex was so still that it was like gazing downward into a deep, untroubled black pool.

Camille had become unconscious. Alf was thankful for that. So long as his strength remained he would hold her; at the last, when it was gone, they would slip quietly into those black depths. They seemed to hypnotise him as he looked down into them.

And of all the things that would have seemed the least probable to Alf was the likelihood that he would die thus, holding Camille in his arms. As he held her he knew that his love for her was eternal; all the pettiness of the past was swept away, and in those moments he became something greater than he had ever been, something he had always wanted to be. And the scheme of his life grew very clear to him, he saw his mother's face, he knew it was to her that he owed that last and greatest discovery of his life . . .

He was being chilled into unconsciousness. He awoke with a start and gazed into Camille's white face. She lay inert in his arms, hardly breathing. Thoughts of rescue sometimes passed through his mind, but he banished them instantly. Bartel? But Charles and the events of recent days had almost slipped from his memory, which was going back toward the past, the city flat, his uncle's farm; even the pen was left behind; nothing that had happened since his mother died seemed to have left any permanent imprint upon him . . .

Again he started. He knew the end could not be far off now. He strained his eyes upward. The moon hung overhead, shining through the cataract, turning it into a thing of unimaginable beauty. Above him was the ledge from which he had fallen. Now, as he stared at it through the spray, he fancied he saw the flash of lanterns.

Dreaming again! He clutched Camille more tightly and looked down, dismissing the vague thoughts of rescue as something that did not concern him, something hardly to be wished for. Far better to die thus, in this drowsy place . . .

He was, in fact, only dimly conscious of the shouts above him. Pascal, Chamberland and Robitaille, roped together, had negotiated the rocky ledge to the end, and were staring down, crossing themselves in terror at the sight of Alf and Camille

341

beneath the waterfall.

The search of the dam for Alf's body not having brought it to light, the three had started up the gorge to find it. It was not until they reached the rollways and saw the heap of sand, and Alf's imprint on the snow, that the thought came to them that he might be alive.

Then they had followed the riverbed, discovering traces of him — here a footprint on snow, there an ice sheet fractured by a heel. So travelling, they had come upon Celeste, seated with Bartel upon the shore.

Charles, who was conscious, had given them a brief, disjointed story of the happenings of the night. They had obtained a long rope from the abandoned camp and made their way along the ledge, without the smallest expectation of finding either of the two.

Alf had just strength and consciousness enough to understand the meaning of the rope that was lowered to him. He made it fast about Camille and himself, and they were drawn up to the ledge.

Where it terminated in the shore Bartel,

supported by Celeste, was standing, staring at something that the current was washing toward the bank.

It was the body of Philippe. A last lap of the stream stranded it among the rocks. Philippe lay there, composed, and, perhaps, more dignified in death than he had ever been when posing as the seigneur of the Destry lands. Charles Bartel stared at it and uttered a cry.

'*Ah, mon Dieu*, it is the face of the slayer whom I saw in the fog!'

* * *

'No, the lands are mademoiselle's. They were *always* mademoiselle's. Monsieur Edouard refused at the last moment to sell, or even to take a mortgage.'

Camille and Alf were seated on the stoop of the Destry home a month later, Sorel, in his long chair, beside them. Camille was convalescing from the long illness that had followed the events of that night. It was the first time the subject had been taken up.

'If I understand you rightly, Monsieur

Sorel,' said Alf, 'you perpetrated this fraud in order to ensure that the lands should go to Mademoiselle Destry — you must forgive my bluntness.'

'Ah, Collet, I spoke to you of our loyalty to the land, but you did not follow me. Why not, monsieur? It is true I had coveted the lands since I was a boy, but Monsieur Edouard would not sell, and in no other way could I have kept them out of — ' He broke off there. He meant Philippe's hands.

'Monsieur Sorel,' said Camille suddenly, 'you know what I have never asked you. But some day I must know the facts. I think, perhaps, it would be better to tell me now. Then we will never speak about the matter again. What happened that night?'

'You are sure you wish me to tell you, mademoiselle? Well, then, as you know, your father and I went to Fall City for the purpose of disposing of the lands. Your brother and your father had quarreled, as you know. Your father had denied his house to him. Your brother was destitute. He considered himself ill-used.

344

'In his desperation, learning that your father was going to Fall City to raise money, he conceived the idea of following him and extorting some from him by some means or other. I learned of it by accident.

'I knew that your brother had been there before, and was acquainted with this man, Egan. I went to see Egan and urged him to watch over Philippe and see that he did neither his father nor himself any harm.

'Egan saw the chance to turn matters to his advantage, as he thought. He soon learned the reason for Monsieur Edouard's visit. He planned to have him murdered for the money he was believed to be carrying.

'Mademoiselle — ' He turned earnestly to Camille. ' — your brother was no intentional murderer. He told me the story in the first wild confession. He waylaid his father with the intention of appealing to him. His father ordered him from his sight for ever. In his despair your brother struck him. Your father fell. He must have fractured his skull upon the curb, for your brother swore to me that he had nothing in his hand. And all the while the men Egan had hired were in waiting.

'Egan used this happening to the full. He used it to send you to the penitentiary, Collet. He used it to keep Charles Bartel away while he ruined his sweetheart — may they be happy where they have gone, for assuredly they were not the least of Egan's victims. He used it as a club over Philippe, driving him to drink until in desperation he was even willing to sell his sister's honour. But he was insane at that time, mademoiselle, and in the end — I am sure — he repented. But over me he held this club to gain a partnership in the lands, to force me to alienate the men by burning their homes — because he knew our *Canayen* loyalty. How could I let my old seigneur's son go to the gallows or the penitentiary?'

'Monsieur Sorel,' said Alf huskily, 'you told me you yourself had murdered Monsieur Destry.'

'Monsieur Collet, I thought you were a detective from the moment I set eyes on you.'

'And you preferred to take the blame?'

Sorel shrugged his shoulders.

'Monsieur Sorel, I misjudged you, I guess,' said Alf.

'Ah, well, everything is as it should be now,' answered Sorel.

'You see,' said Camille to Alf later that evening, 'all that was no news to me. Deep down in me I always knew something like that had happened. It was my fears for Philippe that actuated me in everything I did. Egan knew that, and he played with me as skillfully as any cat with any mouse. He never assuaged my fears by converting them into certainty, so that at least I could face the worst. Always at the bottom of my mind there was this nameless horror, which I would never even admit to myself, that my brother was my father's murderer. If only he had told *me* what he admitted to Monsieur Sorel — '

She broke off and was silent for a while.

'It reached the point where I had to choose between Philippe and you, Alf,' she said. 'Then I made myself hate you. I made myself believe that foolish thing about Celeste, which I never believed. But now — it's all a nightmare, and I remember hardly anything of it.'

'We must never think of it,' said Alf. 'I guess I've got a whole lot to put out of my mind, too.'

'We'll have to help each other,' said Camille.

We do hope that you have enjoyed reading this large print book.

Did you know that all of our titles are available for purchase?

We publish a wide range of high quality large print books including:
**Romances, Mysteries, Classics
General Fiction
Non Fiction and Westerns**

Special interest titles available in large print are:
**The Little Oxford Dictionary
Music Book, Song Book
Hymn Book, Service Book**

Also available from us courtesy of Oxford University Press:
**Young Readers' Dictionary
(large print edition)
Young Readers' Thesaurus
(large print edition)**

For further information or a free brochure, please contact us at:
**Ulverscroft Large Print Books Ltd.,
The Green, Bradgate Road, Anstey,
Leicester, LE7 7FU, England.
Tel:** (00 44) **0116 236 4325
Fax:** (00 44) **0116 234 0205**

LORD JAMES HARRINGTON AND THE SPRING MYSTERY

Lynn Florkiewicz

James and his wife Beth are hosting the annual spring fair when wealthy recluse Delphine Brooks-Hunter is murdered. While James is summoned to the reading of her will and is tasked with solving an intriguing riddle, Beth tackles her own mystery after discovering a homeless man suffering from amnesia. As they delve deeper, a number of questions emerge. What links Delphine to the fairground folk? Who would harm such a refined lady? Are rumours of wartime espionage true? As they unravel the truth, they uncover more than they bargained for . . .

LORD JAMES HARRINGTON AND THE SUMMER MYSTERY

Lynn Florkiewicz

It's summer, and the annual tennis tournament between Cavendish and Charnley is underway; but a sudden spate of jewel thefts prompts James to put his sleuthing hat on. His investigation suggests that the criminals are using an ancient smuggling network. Can he convince his good friend, DCI George Lane, of his suspicions? Is the murder of the tennis umpire connected? Could a long-term resident really be a criminal mastermind? James desperately struggles for answers as he explores hidden tunnels, studies old maps and examines the motives of his fellow villagers.

THE RED TAPE MURDERS

Gerald Verner

Superintendent Budd's latest murder investigation begins with the murder of a solicitor, found strangled with red tape. Soon, two more local solicitors are murdered in similar fashion. Eventually Budd learns that two years earlier, a man shot himself when about to lose the bungalow he built, under a compulsory purchase order of the council. Two of the solicitors had acted in the sale of the land, and the third had acted for the council. Is someone seeking vengeance for the man who committed suicide — himself a victim of red tape?

GHOST LAKE

V. J. Banis

Its real name is Caspar Lake, but people call it Ghost Lake. Years ago, a ferryboat went down in a storm, drowning everyone on board — and some say their souls have never rested . . . Beth Nolan travels to the nearby town at the invitation of an old school friend, but no sooner does she arrive than she is plunged into the murky depths of the brutal murder of a young woman. Beth must find answers — or risk joining the dead in the haunted depths of Ghost Lake . . .